Projection

By Tabatha Shipley

Copyright © 2019 Tabatha Shipley
Cover by Abeni Trotter

ISBN 9781699851647

Because of the dynamic nature of the Internet, any web addresses or links contained in this book may have changed since publication and may no longer be valid.

For information, email tabatha@tabathashipleybooks.com

Also by Tabatha Shipley:

Kingdom of Fraun Series

Breaking Eselda

Redeeming Jordyn

30 Days Without Wings

Chapter 1

—◆— — —◆— — —◆— — —◆— — —◆— — —◆— — —◆— — —◆— — —◆— — —◆— — —◆—

A QUICK GLANCE at my watch tells me how late I really am. 8:13. That's not a little late, like you missed roll call. That's like teacher-already-started-her-lesson late. I'm tempted to turn right instead of left. Take solace in the coffeehouse since I'm already tardy. Instead, I run in my stupid knee high boots that I wore to impress my recently ex-boyfriend, Tyler. Outside the classroom I take a deep breath before turning the handle. I'm just wondering how lucky I really am; maybe Mrs. Straightier won't be looking at the door.

I hold the handle still and ease the door closed until it clicks. My eyes take in the teacher in the center of the carved out bowl that makes up the classroom. An image from the 20th century fills the screen behind her. The large room is about three-quarters full of glossy-eyed students desperately trying to act like they care about History.

I silently slink into the chair at the back row, closest to the door. I close my eyes tight and hold my breath. Did I make it?

"Miss Johnson, please rise."

Crap. I didn't make it. I stand shakily to my feet. My eyes are plastered to the concrete flooring as I await my fate. I can hear the sniggering around me. My classmates will wallow in the pain and misery of anyone who is not them like a pig will wallow in mud, or something worse. I wish I could flip them all off.

"Miss Johnson, please regale us with your tale of why you neglected to join us on time for the third day this week."

"I overslept." I risk a glance at the front board. Sure enough her projection has gone black; she's no longer focused on her lesson.

"Excuse me? What was that? Please speak up."

"I overslept," I repeat, a bit louder.

"Miss Johnson, please cast your eyes to the front."

I pull my eyes to the large white board at the front of the room. Mrs. Straightier is standing just below it. The room is designed like all other classrooms, with the board high up on the salmon colored wall. The board is designed especially for projections.

She crosses to the right hand side of the room, her high heels tapping out what is probably Morse code for 'I hate tardies.' Her fingers tap the small metal projection plate, but her eyes remain glued to the room full of kids. I can feel them boring a hole in my forehead. They gloss ever-so-slightly before my attention is diverted to the board with the projection.

The scene is the classroom. Mrs. Straightier must be focused on the clock, because our projection begins with it filling the screen, proudly displaying 7:55. We pan out to view the entire class. Every seat is full, including mine. We are all seated. Not only are we seated, we are sitting up straight with our feet delicately crossed at the ankles staring up at her with Stepford Wife style smiles on our faces. Frankly, it's disgusting.

"Well, class. It appears that we are all present and ready five minutes early. Let us begin," Mrs. Straightier, the projection, says from her position at the front of the room.

The projection fades. "Are we clear?" The real Mrs. Straightier is louder, snarkier. Somehow it comes across as scarier. This is the version of Mrs. Straightier who will rip your head from your shoulders for disrupting her lesson plan.

"Yes ma'am." I'm relieved when the entire class answers with me.

Chapter 2

"EMMA, WAIT UP!" The bellowing voice of my best friend, Bella, stops me in my steps. I slide my hand into the back pocket of my jeans and pull out my phone. Bella always sits toward the front of the classroom. It's fine for her, but it means you really have to wait for her to get all the way to the top of the stairs among the crowd of students exiting the room.

I pull over in the hallway, leaning my shoulder against the stucco covered brick and open my Rubik's app. I've been trying to learn how to solve the virtual four by four cube. You know, because I need another basically useless talent to wait for someone to bring up at a party or something.

"Emma, oh my gawd, you missed it." Bella pulls up alongside me and links our elbows to effectively pull me into the corridor. Excellent. If she's going to steer, I'm gonna keep playing. "Missed what?" I ask, head still down.

"Marcus actually spoke to me. We had actual contact," Bella says.

"What did he say?"

"Let me show you." She motions for my phone. I switch the phone to my other hand and tilt it toward Bella. Then I raise my eyebrows at my blonde bombshell of a best friend. She has been obsessed with our football star, Marcus, since he almost ran her over in the hall freshman year. Somehow I seriously doubt they magically had a moment today.

Bella taps my phone screen. The message appears. *Annabella Norte is attempting to send communication.* I hit accept.

I'm looking down at a desk not unlike the one I just vacated. The difference is I'm obviously seated at someone else's desk because my desk is certainly not taken up by a spiral notebook filled with post-it flags in various colors. There are five different colored highlighters alongside the notebook. This is Bella's desk. The projection's focus shifts to the left, to a backpack. A noise from the other side causes the projection to shift immediately to the right.

The notebook now lays in the center aisle of the classroom. I watch as Bella's hand reaches out toward it, perfectly manicured pink shiny nails coming just short.

She shifts in her seat, I can tell because this time her little arm comes closer. A pair of black running shoes stops in our line of sight. The projection slides up his muscular arm to reveal Marcus, the boy Bella is seriously crushing on. Dark, dangerous looking Marcus with his overly ripped abs and pecs.

He smiles and I hear Bella giggle. He hands her the notebook. "Is this yours?" he asks in his deep baritone.

"It... um... yeah... thanks."

Smooth, Bella.

Her hand wraps around the notebook.

"Can you believe it? Isn't he the best?" Bella asks. The screen returns to showing my app.

"Bella, he hardly talked to you at all."

"Did he or did he not take his time to hand me my notebook?" She shoves her skinny little hip out and plants her hand on it. Her sparkling blue eyes are wide open, challenging me.

I sigh, mostly because I don't want to have this argument. "He did."

"Exactly. So it's better than your morning." We are pulling up to my next classroom. Bella slows and drops my arm. "You can't argue with that, Emma."

"No, I certainly can't."

"Why were you late anyway?" she asks.

"My Dad's stupid invention didn't work." My father, the great Steve Johnson, is an inventor. He works with computers and technology and other stuff I don't really understand. He was one of the people to help modify the old NFC chip for human implants.

His newest project isn't nearly as cool. He's trying to design some kind of slow release wake up technique that mimics the rising sun on the wall of your room. It's supposed to allow you to wake up "naturally." I don't know why you couldn't just install a glass wall and wake up with the real sun.

Anyway, it didn't work. Well technically I guess it did. The machine projected a rising sun on my wall slowly and, probably, beautifully. What it didn't do is wake me up. Dad came in hollering at me for running late and "not appreciating technology" with something resembling full noon sunlight taking up my bedroom wall.

"All you have to do is set your phone to wake you. Problem solved." Bella taps my screen again. *Annabella Norte is attempting to send communication.* "Seriously? Turn it off private while you're at it."

"Then everyone could send me any projection they want. That's dumb, Bells." Accept.

On my screen Bella walks me through the steps to setting an alarm. Next she runs me through the keystrokes that would turn my setting to 'public.'

"Bella, I knew how to do all that. I'm not a total idiot," I whine.

"Well then, no excuses. Hey, I gotta run to class. Talk soon!" Bella is off down the hall without waiting to for me to awkwardly say bye.

I can't think of any acceptable reasons to be late to the class I'm standing outside of, so I turn and head inside.

Chapter 3

THERE'S THIS COFFEE shop we hit up on our way home from school sometimes. It's a block away from the High School, it has free projection screens, and they don't rush you out of the building. So, you know, perfect. Once, during final exam season, they even offered you free drinks if you could prove you were studying. After my crappy morning being late to History I had an exam in Math and a presentation in Literature. Yeah, I could use a coffee.

I command my music player and the sounds of Local Evolution fill my ears. This technology, the one that allows me to listen to music through my nervous chip, was not Dad's idea. Some other guy in the company figured that part out. Totally cool. I bet his daughter doesn't have the virtual sun shining on her bedroom wall.

The coffee shop is pretty packed today. There are fifteen tables and two projection screens in the little shop. Today, although most of the tables are full, both screens are showing the swirling logo of the Half Cup.

I step into the line. Standing still now I can really feel the sweat droplets running down my neck and back, it's disgusting. I twirl my hair up into a bun and pull it like a knot. It stays up, meaning I probably need a haircut. But at least it's off my neck as I wait in line. I can see a few other kids from the school sitting around the shop. I always wonder how the heck people manage to beat me over here. Some of them even have coffee already. Do they, like, skip eighth period?

The guy in front of me orders, pays with change (yawn) and finally steps out of the way. I think about my music turning down and it complies. "Hi, can I get an iced mocha without whipped cream, please?"

"What size, honey?"

I hate when they call you honey. I give her what I hope is a contemptuous glare. "Big."

"You got it. Name?"

"Emma."

"Perfect. That will be six eighty-three, Emma." She hits me with a perfect smile, tilting her head to the right. It's off putting. You'd think I would be used to perfect. My best friend is a perky blonde with perfect teeth. She is absolutely gorgeous. Of course she also happens to be insanely smart and dedicated to her studies. Apparently, that's a complete turn off to men. Whatever.

I mentally command the pay app to open. The preloaded cash balance from my parents flashes on the screen briefly before I tap the payment plate. I'm not old enough to have a bank account so these preloaded gift cards are the only way I can pay, for now. The beep tells me it registered. I twirl before the barista can offer me a receipt and take the first open seat I see. It puts me near the counter facing the line of windows out to the street. My music turns back up and I try to ignore my own image shining back in my phone's reflection. I am not perfect. My brown hair lays straight, my brown eyes scream boring, and my nose is too big. I don't even have supersmart going for me. Perfect Bella and Average Emma, that's us.

My screen flashes a picture of Bella and I, arms wrapped around each other's shoulders and smiling. I didn't command a picture of us. Did I? I was sitting here thinking about how different we are, but I didn't actually call up a picture. Did I? This is weird.

I turn my phone over and take out the battery. I wipe it on my shirt and slide it back in. I focus on calling up my coffee order. The video starts.

There I am at the coffee counter again. The condescending cashier smiling at me. She gets closer because I stepped forward. Here comes my order. "Hi, can I get an iced mocha without whipped cream, please?"

The screen fades back to black showing my perplexed grimace in the reflection. Seems to be working fine. That was exactly what I called up. So what was with the picture? I put the phone down and tap my right wrist. Somewhere deep under there is a small chip that connects to my nervous system and allows me to interact with all this technology. Maybe there's a problem with--

"Iced mocha, no whip," the barista calls from the counter behind me.

I turn and raise my hand in the classic "that's mine, don't give it to anyone else" gesture. I notice, as I walk to grab it, that my music has stopped. That's the one downfall of all this technology focused on your brain, it all knows when you've stopped paying attention to it. It's worse

16

than babysitting; it needs constant attention or it fades. No longer do we listen to music or watch TV in the background, like I clearly remember doing when I was tiny. Nope, you have to be focused on that crap or it fades. I call up the song again as my hand wraps around the cup. "Thank you." I smile. The barista nods once in acknowledgement.

Beside me a projection screen comes to life and draws my attention. Is that my History classroom? I take my seat again but keep watching the replay. Sure enough, it's my class. There's my teacher, standing in her little bowl at the front of the room. Who is watching this? I look around and find two boys I recognize. Tom Martin and Chris White. The Chris White. The Chris White who exudes confidence and swag with every breath he takes. The Chris White who plays some sport other people care about and has a letter jacket to prove it. The Chris White who doesn't know I'm alive.

On the screen the point of view turns to take in the door. It's slowly opening. Why are we watching a projection of someone slipping into History late? Oh no. Yup, that's my leg entering through the door. There's the rest of me. Oh man.

"Miss Johnson, please rise." Yup I remember that line. I watch myself stand up. I notice the projection bounces a little. I guess I know who was laughing.

The POV shifts back to the front of the room. It stays there, on Mrs. Straightier, for a second. Then it turns to the right. There's a girl leaning over toward something she must have dropped. She's trying to reach under the row of chairs in front of her. Her whole body is contorted basically in half as she stretches. Whoever's projection we are watching is enraptured because her black thong is hanging out over the top of her jeans, poor girl. He taps the kid sitting on his right side and gestures to the thong. It earns him a thumbs up.

"Dude, is that Marcy Wakeman?" Tom asks as the screen goes back to the coffee house logo.

"The one-and-only," Chris answers.

Marcy Wakeman is also a perky blonde. The difference between her and Bella is that Marcy Wakeman does not have the smarts which are man kryptonite. She's that girl that every high school has. The one that everyone half hates and half envies. Still, I feel sorry for her that she showed her underwear to everyone during history.

"Who's the girl that was late?" Tom asks.

I wish I could hide. This is a public screen they are using. Anyone else in the coffee shop could've been watching, like I was. People now know I was embarrassingly late to History. Of course that embarrassment was overshadowed by Marcy Wakeman's thong, but still.

"Emma Johnson," Chris says.

Wait just one second. Chris White knows my name?

"Well thank you Emma Johnson for being late to class, amIright?" Tom offers his palm to Chris and they high five.

I'm seriously tempted to walk over and tell them both they're welcome. Instead I lean back into my coffee house wooden chair and quickly record the memory to my phone. Then I open a text message. To: Annabelle Norte. "Hey Bells, guess who knows I'm alive???" I attach the video and hit send.

Two sips of mocha later my phone dings. "OMG Emma. You got coffee without me?"

Have I mentioned my best friend's priorities are WAY out of whack sometimes? Reply. "Um that is what you took from this vid? Honey, CHRIS freaking WHITE knew my name. Besides, aren't you at field hockey?"

This time I only have time for one sip. "Yeah... but you still owe me a skinny vanilla."

Another sip. "Ems are we forgetting about Tyler? Just wondering."

Ugh. Tyler. Tyler is my on-again, off-again, on-again, currently off-again boyfriend sort of thing. He is totally adorable. He is sweet like peach cobbler. I wonder if this shop has that. Probably not this time of year. Anyway, Tyler is funny and super amazing. We have known each other for years, practically forever. But no matter how many times we try, it always just ends up that we are terrible at being together romantically.

Most recently I ended it. Tyler had planned this entire date night. We were going to go to the movies then go play miniature golf. I hate miniature golf. I went along with it because Tyler planned it. Somewhere around the fifth hole as I was trying to understand why it was so damn important to get the stupid yellow ball into the opening, Tyler started to lose patience with me. "Just pick it up, Emma. We'll play through."

I kind of lost my temper. "I don't want to play through. This game is stupid." I picked up my yellow ball and whipped it as far as I could. I'm not very sporty, so we could still see it. Just a sad yellow dot taunting me from the lush green fake lawn. You can't even golf right, Emma.

"I'll just go get it, Em. You calm down. Then we'll keep playing." He actually walked off to go get it.

I remember yelling at him. *"It's like you don't even know me at all!"*

The sound of my voice resonates around me like I'm standing in a tunnel. Did my voice just echo through the coffee shop?

No, it couldn't have. That's impossible.

So why is it eerily quiet in here? Even the coffee foamers have gone silent.

Slowly the noise starts to tiptoe back in. There are a few giggles. I'm sitting close enough to hear Tom and Chris resume their conversation.

"Did you hear that?" Tom asks.

"Some girl was ripping into some poor dude," Chris answers. "Where did it come from?"

"Somewhere behind you."

My stomach churns. I'm sitting behind them. I flick my eyes down to my phone. The screen is showing a frozen image of a golf course. A golf course? I was thinking about the golf course. I was thinking about what I yelled at Tyler. What I yelled at Tyler that I thought I heard in the coffee shop instead of in my memory.

I wasn't trying to call up that memory. I didn't send it to the screen, I'm sure of it. What the hell is going on?

Chapter 4

I **HAVE TO** just bite the bullet and do it. Sure, he's not the easiest person to talk to. Sure, he lives in a land where people are responsible and dedicated and he thinks I'm immature and flippant. Sure, he's probably working and therefore unapproachable. This could blow up in my face. But I have to do it. No one else will believe me. No one else will be able to explain it away.

I step forward and knock on the heavy wooden door to my father's study. "Daddy?" May as well shamelessly suck up.

"Come on in." Dad's voice floats cheerfully through the door. This could be a good sign.

He's sitting at his desk but his fingers are nowhere near the keyboard. A book is open in front of him. He offers me a smile that crinkles around the corners of his blue-gray eyes. "What can I do for you, Emma?"

"Um, actually, I had some questions about the NFC chips," I say.

"Really?" His eyes sparkle. He loves when I ask about his work.

I take a seat across the big oak desk from him. He shuts the book and gives me his full attention. "Tell me again how they work," I begin.

"Emma, you know how they work."

I stay silent. Mostly I don't know what to ask. How do I explain what happened in the coffee shop?

Dad sighs. "I'll humor you, I suppose. There is an NFC chip implanted in the wrist of everyone who wants one, which is practically everyone. The old technology allowed you to communicate with something else that contained the chip as long as they were close together. The chip was modified for implants that communicate with your nervous system. That means your nervous system can now communicate with anything that contains the NFC chip; from cell phones to projector plates."

"But we need to command the communication, right?" I ask.

"Yes. The communication command has to be initiated in the nervous system and accepted by the technology."

"Have they ever, like, malfunctioned?"

Dad props his elbow on the desk and rests his chin in the palm. Two of his fingers reach toward his lips. His right eye closes a bit more than his left. "Malfunctioned?"

"Yeah, like, made a mistake." It's clear this is not getting through. "Like in trials and stuff. Did they ever send the wrong memory or send something without the mental command?"

"No. That would not be possible."

"Are you sure?"

"Emma, what is this about?"

Here goes nothing. "My phone kind of brought up a picture that I didn't ask for. I was thinking about it, but I didn't ask for it. Then it did the same thing with a memory I was recalling. It just picked up the memory and projected it without me telling it to. Is that, like, possible?"

"Show me." Dad gestures to the computer monitor on his desk.

I focus on the strange picture first. Then I tap the computer, mentally deciding to share the image.

The scene is like a watery coffee house. Because my mind in this memory is thinking about something besides the present, the reality is distorted. The people of the shop are like shadows, with no distinguishing features. If I hadn't lived the moment I'd be hard pressed to identify the location.

Clearly an image of my face in my phone reflects back to me. The image grows until it is clear and taking up the full screen of the monitor it's playing back on. My hair suddenly appears more oily. Then my eyes darken a little. My nose actually grows. This is how I see myself.

A picture of Bella and I side-by-side fills the phone screen which is occupying most of the computer screen. Bella is in her field hockey uniform, smiling her beautiful smile. I'm sweating from sitting in the stands at her game. Our arms are wrapped around each other.

You can tell, if you look around the phone at the rest of the coffee shop, that we have returned to reality. It is crystal clear. We watch as I shake the phone. I take out the battery and wipe it off.

"That's it. Did you notice?" I ask.

Dad is giving his curious expression to the computer now. "You were touching the phone so communications were possible. Are you absolutely positive you didn't call up that picture?"

"Yes. I was thinking about us, obviously, but I wasn't even

thinking about that particular shot."

"You mentioned a second piece of evidence?"

I mentally decide to share the more embarrassing memory.

Again we are living in my memory. It plays, clearly, over the background of the watery and shadowy coffee shop. We watch my mini golf date from hell with Tyler. I try not to watch, actually. The screen looks darker as I get angry at the fifth hole. It's very dark by the time I pitch the ball.

"You calm down. Then we'll keep playing." As I hear Tyler's voice I take note of it. It sounds like it's only happening inside my head, my memory. It's flat. Quiet.

"It's like you don't even know me at all."

That voice is different. In the video it's obvious, what I missed the first time. The sound of my voice came from the phone in my hand. It is loud, multi-dimensional. It rings throughout the suddenly sharp lines of the coffee shop.

The silent coffee shop. Even on the video the silence is embarrassing.

When noise starts back up the POV focuses on Tom and Chris, whispering over their table. "Did you hear that?"

"Where did it come from?"

"Behind you."

"I was sitting behind them. At the time I didn't know my phone did it. But in the vision, you could tell. Right?"

"Yes. The chip in your phone picked up your memory and relayed it," Dad answers.

"Is that normal?" The silence stretches. He's not going to answer me. He's deep in science-man mode. You can almost see the smoke rising out of his ears as he gives the computer that crooked squint of his.

"No," he says.

I jump at the sound of Dad's voice.

"Let me show you something."

It's this conversation, from Dad's POV. I'm on the other side of the table looking at myself. Well, a rather far-fetched version of myself. My hair is not that glossy, Dad.

The image gets watery and a flash of something fills the screen.

"Did you see that?" real world Dad asks.

"That flash? Yeah, what was that?"

"That was the memory I was getting ready to share. It flashed in my mind before I called it up to show you. Watch again, I will freeze it this time." He puts his hands over the keyboard. "Ready?"

I nod, my eyes fixed on the screen.

There's me, looking a bit nervous.

The image gets watery again, meaning we are entering Dad's memories.

The screen flash freezes.

I risk a look at Dad. He smiles and points to the screen. "What do you see, Em? It's a frozen scene from that projection."

It's the exact me I saw at the beginning of his projection. Frozen and full of color and life.

"That's where the projection started," I say.

"Exactly. In order to command a projection to start, the nervous system will flash upon the projection briefly. You would have to know what you are looking for, or be very quick with the pause, to see it."

"But you didn't see that flash in my projections?"

"No. In fact it seemed as though your projection of the golf game actually came simultaneously with your memory. It should've been after." Dad rubs the back of his neck and stares down at his desk. "Of course, projections are faulty because they are based on our brains, which are not at all perfect. We remember colors and conversation wrong, we remember emotions differently. We can manufacture or alter memories by thinking about them enough. For this reason, it is possible that flash happened but you didn't show me in the projection because you aren't adept at noticing them." Dad sits back in his chair. "In fact, I'm sure that's what happened." He smiles. "This, although strange, is probably nothing, Emma. You didn't focus on sending the image, but you must have sent it."

"What should I do then? That was embarrassing, Dad."

"Nothing. I know you were embarrassed, but this is not the technology that let you down. You called up that memory, you just didn't realize you did it."

"But--"

"Emma, be serious. You are just mortified that this happened to you and you are looking for something or someone to blame. Be more careful with what you choose to send to your phone in the future." Dad reopens the book, dropping it to the center of the desk with a thump. Conversation over.

Dad is right, I'm sure. He would know better than anyone how these chips work. I must have called up that memory, I just can't remember doing it. I'll be more careful and it will never happen again.

Right?

Chapter 5

---·——·——·——·———·———·———·———·———·———·——·—

WHAT IS THAT noise? The chirping comes again. To my blissfully sleep-filled ears, the sound is painful. I squeeze my eyes shut tighter, willing the misery to stop.

I think it's my phone.

It's dark in my room because I was smart enough to turn off the virtual wall, so I have to fumble for the phone. I keep my eyes closed. I think I read somewhere that my other senses should be heightened if one is not being used, or something.

My hand connects with the rectangle and I bring it up to my ear, swiping with my thumb to unlock. Hopefully I don't have the thing upside down. "Hello?"

"Good morning, Emma," Bella sings. "Are you awake? I wouldn't want you to be late to school."

"What time is it?"

"7:30."

Crap! "Seriously Bells?" I sit up in bed. By 7:30 I should already be headed out of the house. I should already be dressed. I should already have eaten something.

"Yes, ma'am. Can you get your rear down here, please? I can't have you in detention tonight. I have a game."

"I'll be there, I promise. Hey, Bells…"

"Yes?"

"You're the best. Thank you."

"Welcome."

I hear the click that tells me Bella has disconnected and I do the same. I fight that strange urge to lay back down. The one that says, "oh you're already going to be late why not make it worth it." I fight right through it and run to my closet. I don't even think about being alluring or aloof, I just grab clothes and throw them on. I'm actually hopping into my sneakers as I race out the front door. I know, I know… could I be more cliché?

After a mad dash to the high school, which is exactly 0.9 miles from my house according to a search I once did during free period, it's officially 7:58. You know what that means? I might actually make it.

By the time I turn the corner into the hallway of my History class, goal in sight, she is trying to close the classroom door. "I'm here," I gasp. I hope she understood, I'm seriously out of breath.

"Miss Johnson." She checks her watch. "Technically you are on time. Congratulations," Mrs. Straightier says. "Come in. Sit." She shuts the door behind us.

Now I'm glad I am on time, trust me on that. Bella was absolutely right, one more tardy and my sorry butt would be in detention after school today. But I'm also the idiot gasping for breath at the back of the classroom with sweat dripping down my face like the condensation on an iced coffee I didn't have time to get. In this day and age that's fodder for embarrassing memory videos later. Story of my life, I guess.

I crumple into the back row empty seat and pull out a spiral notebook. I flip to a blank page, set a pen beside it, and then lay my phone on top. Mrs. Straightier's heels click down the center stairs and I bring my eyes to her once they stop. "Today we will be continuing our discussion on the reformation of the Eurasian Union in the early 21st century."

I live in the United States. More specifically, I live in Arizona. So I fail to see what learning about the unionization of some of the countries of Asia and Europe have to do with me. Then again, I can name all 197 countries in the world and that doesn't really have anything to do with me either. I'm full of useless skills.

I touch my phone around the same time Mrs. Straightier touches the projection plate on the wall and brings up an image of the world map zoomed in around the Eurasian Union. I pull up a History channel article about the issue and skim through it. I click through the links that bring me information about the USSR, the Cold War, and the price of the Euro throughout the years. My personal conclusions; people need to stop assuming everyone will make the same mistake twice. The European Union has been in place for like fifty years now and all they've done is increase trade and economy in those countries.

Satisfied that I successfully learned everything I need about this merger, I open a game of cards.

"Not interested in History?"

I turn my attention to the voice on my left. I don't recognize this guy. He's cute so I would remember. Dark hair cut short, faint mustache forming on the upper lip, and blue eyes that remind me of the summer sky. "I just don't think lecture is always the only way to learn," I whisper.

"How do you prefer to learn?" cloudless sky eyes asks.

I shake my phone. "Research."

"You read a few articles and you are an expert?"

"No. I read a few articles and I have both sides. I make opinions. What's to say Mrs. Staightier planned on bringing us both sides?" I answer.

He shrugs. "Fair point." He holds out his hand. "I'm Alex. Alex Slater."

Alex Slater has quite a grip, let me tell you. "I'm Emma Johnson."

"Nice to meet you Emma." Alex's attention slips back to the front of the room. I glance down at his notebook. He has a full page of notes in a slanted careful handwriting. They are bulleted like an outline and incredibly formal. Organized guy, this Alex.

I look down to take stock of the outfit I chose in my hurry this morning. The jeans are my old favorites. The ones that fit just right and are faded just enough. The perfect kind of flirting jeans. The shirt is a probably clean pink cotton that I picked up off the floor. There are no stains, so that's good. I run my hands down the stomach area to flatten out the few wrinkles. My sneakers, which are still untied, are running shoes. I guess it works with the ponytail I hastily threw together. Maybe Alex will think I wake up early to run or something. Maybe that's why I'm always late to school. It's a way better story than the reality. I grab my pen and scratch out a few of the things I learned during my research, in case he's looking.

"Emma," Alex whispers.

I turn my head. He's still facing forward, but his mouth has curled up in a smile like a secret. My heart flutters a little. "Alex?" I try to match his tone.

"Do you like coffee?" he asks.

"Yes." What is he implying? Oh my gosh, am I getting ahead of this? Is he asking me out for coffee? Breathe, Emma.

"Would you like to grab a coffee after school and share both sides of the issue with me?" He turns his head just a little. Just enough to allow me to see both eyes, then he snaps them back to the front again.

I swear my breath is stuck in my throat.

"Sure." Think of something witty. Memorable. Cute. "I wouldn't want you to only have one side of the issue." YES!

Alex chuckles. It's like this cute little half laugh sound that bubbles up out of his gray t-shirt. "I can meet you out front after school. We can walk to Half Cup, if you want," he offers.

"Great. I'll be there."

"That's the end of our time, ladies and gentlemen. Please be ready for a quiz tomorrow on the topic of Eurasia." Mrs. Straightier has impeccable timing. She calls this out just as I hear the bell begin toning.

"See you after school, Emma," Alex says. He hits me with a melt-your-heart kind of smile and disappears into the sea of kids flowing out the open door behind me.

I stay glued to my seat waiting for Bella to pack up her extensive materials and bounce her way up the aisle. I stand up when I see her drawing close. "Bella, guess what?"

"What?"

"I have a coffee date." I do a little mini dance as we leave the room.

Bella smacks me on the shoulder. "No way! With who? When? I'm so excited."

"His name is Alex Slater. He was sitting next to me in History. He asked me to get coffee. Look, look. Isn't he cute?"

I pull up the memory of Alex, first his generally-interested-in-what-I'm-doing expression. Then that switches for the little half smile. Finally, I hit her with the endearing chuckle.

Bella hops up and down beside me. "He is adorable! Why don't I know him?"

"Maybe he's new, I'm not sure. I'm so excited. We are getting coffee after school today. Get this, he said he would meet me out front and walk me there..." My voice trails off because Bella is no longer beside me. I stop walking and turn my head. Yup, there she is. She's like three steps behind me, staring at me. "Bells, what's going on?"

"Did you say today?"

"Yes." What is her problem? Why would she...? The memory crashes like a wave and I rush to her. "Oh my gosh, Bella I completely forgot. I will cancel the date. I will be at your game, I swear. What time is the game? Bella, it was an accident, believe me."

"You're at all of my games, Emma. You're like good luck. I need you there. Please," Bella says. Her eyes are filling with tears. It makes me feel like a total heel.

"I will be there." I touch her arm gently. "I just forgot for a second. Alex will totally understand, Bells. I promise I will be there."

Bella smiles. "Thanks, Emma. I'm sorry I'm so weird about this. It's just that there's no one else who comes." Bella's parents are disconnected. Mom is a major shopper and Dad is a workaholic. I'm literally all she has.

"I know. It's not a big deal. I want to be there, honest." The thing is, I really do. I mean, I want to be on a date with Alex Slater too, but not instead of this. Maybe he'll be up for drinking coffee tomorrow. Maybe he likes field hockey.

      Who knows?

Chapter 6

"HEY EMMA," TYLER greets. He drops down in the uncomfortable high-backed chair next to me at our table in Math. He always sits here once he thinks we are okay. It's a sign that he is over our latest break-up debacle.

I take a quick look around the room. There are empty seats elsewhere. I decide on a friendly tone as easily as someone would choose what shoes to wear. "Hi Tyler. How are things?" I ask. I take note of his clothes; jeans, ripped a little in that on-purpose way, white t-shirt, black sneakers. His brown hair's a mess, but it looks intentional. Like sticking up out of his head and held there with some kind of gel. This is not the get-my-attention look following our break-ups. This is moved on city. Then again I suppose you could say the same thing about my running shoes getup.

"Things are good. Can we talk about Bella?" he asks.

"Sure." The three of us have always been kind of close. Tyler was in our third grade class and he just kind of stuck around. Although he dates me off and on, because he's adorable, Bella and Tyler are like brother and sister. He is uber protective.

"Class is gonna start. Can I just send you the video she sent me? You can explain your side to me after class, yeah?" His words kind of tumble out. He hits me with this kind of concerned expression, his brown eyes begging for truth.

I try to ignore the flip-floppy feeling in my gut at meeting those eyes. They are, for sure, his best feature. Not oceans like Alex. Tyler has eyes like chocolate mousse.

"Yeah, okay." I have no idea what this could be about. Suddenly, I'm nervous. Is Bella like, into Tyler? Is that why she asked me about him yesterday? How would I feel about Bella and Tyler? My mind swirls with memories of times we were all together. Maybe I missed something? I hold my phone out to Tyler and he taps it.

Tyler Garfield is attempting to send communication. Accept.

POV: a classroom. Likely History, again. There's me, in today's outfit. The POV is drawing closer to me. Okay, I'm Bella.

"Bella, guess what?" projection me asks. Man, my voice sounds weird.

"What?" Yup, Bella.

"I have a coffee date." That dance looked ridiculous. Mental note: do not do that dance again.

Real life me is blushing. Tyler saw this? Okay that is awkward. Why would Bella send Tyler a video memory of me talking about my date? I risk a glance at him. His bushy eyebrows are tugged together and he is furiously scribbling in his notebook. He's either not paying attention to me or he's faking it for the sake of Mr. Richter. Back to the video.

The POV is watching my phone show images of Alex. My heart flutters. What a cutie. The image starts to bob. "He is adorable! Why don't I know him?" *Bella's voice comes from off screen.*

"He's new. I'm so excited. We are getting coffee after school today. He's meeting me out front and walking me..." *I hear my voice but it gets further away as Bella stops in her tracks. The entire screen gets a bit darker. Bella is probably scrunching her little blue eyes at me. Screen me stops and turns around. Confusion crosses my face.* "Bells, what's going on?"

"Did you say today?"

"Yes." *There's a pause, as I realize my mistake. Then I rush to her.* "Bells, I'm sorry, I forgot. I really want to go on this date though. You understand, right?"

Wait, that is not what I said. Is it?

"You're at all my games, Emma. You're like good luck. I need you there. Please," *Bella begs. The screen wavers a little under the filter of her tears.*

"I'm sorry Bells. I just can't pass this up." *I hear my voice saying it. I see my mouth moving like it's what I said. But it's NOT what I said!*

"I'm sorry I'm so weird about this, Emma. It's just that there's no one else who comes."

"I know. I'm sorry."

The projection ends, my phone returns to the home screen. My jaw is probably lying on the table. I scribble on my notebook. "Tyler, I swear this is not how that went down. Watch." I tap him on the arm and show him what I wrote.

He puts his hand out for my phone. I call up the memory and hand it to him. He turns his body slightly to watch my version of the memory. I can't see it over his shoulder and I don't want to draw attention to our inattention, so I focus on the teacher.

My mind wanders. Why would Bella remember me asking her permission to miss her game for my date? I did the exact opposite. I promised her it meant the world to me and swore I'd cancel my date. That was like two periods ago. How did she have time to analyze it enough to alter her memory of it in that time? I know two people often remember situations differently, but this is ridiculous.

Tyler hands my phone back to me. There's a typed message on the screen. It's a text from me, but it hasn't been sent. Tyler must have typed it. It's a message for Bella.

I read it. "Bells I will be at the game! YAY!"

He is looking at me, waiting to see what I think. I'm torn between Tyler's easy way out and my own brand of justice, which would've included pointing out that she is wrong. In the end, it's an easy call. Tyler is a nice guy, it's what is most endearing about him. It's something I should probably strive for more of.

I hit send.

The teacher in this class, Mr. Richter, always assigns partner work toward the end of the class period. I sit there, tapping my foot and waiting through most of his class period for him to announce it. I watch him scribble examples on the board, talk through an explanation, and pace the front of the room like his leash is tethered to the podium. "Alright, pair up and complete the assignment on the board," he calls. Finally!

I grab Tyler's arm before he can even think about ditching me for someone else. "What was up with that video memory?" I ask. I have the afterthought to open my textbook to the appropriate page and write my name on a sheet of notebook paper.

"Bella was upset. She said you were ditching her for some date. I didn't believe her," Tyler says. I try to ignore what looks like hurt in his eyes. That must be my imagination. He's in his moved-on clothes. "She sent me the video to prove it." He shrugs and starts writing out problem number one on his own lined paper.

"But you watched my video, right? I never said I was ditching her. I just forgot she had a game tonight. I'm going to the game."

"I know, I saw." Tyler continues to write.

I watch his careful handwriting line up number after number. He finishes the first one, boxes the answer, and writes the number two. "Ty, do you believe me?" I ask.

"Does it matter? You're going. It'll all blow over when you show up. She won't even remember all this tomorrow."

"I guess." I pull my eyes to the textbook. The math equations kind of swim on the page. There's a lot of letters in there. "What are we even solving for?" I ask.

"We're just reworking the equations to rewrite for y," Tyler answers without looking up.

"So like y equals... whatever? Not a solution?"

"You can't solve them, you don't have enough information." He moves his paper toward me to show me what he's done for problem one.

"Okay." I let my brain process the math. It keeps me from over-analyzing Bella's memory video. I manage to solve the first one and move onto the second one. By the time I'm on question four I'm actually feeling pretty confident.

"So, Alex Slater?" Tyler prompts.

"What?" Completely immersed as I am in the world of algebra, it takes a second to pull myself back to reality. "What about him?" I ask.

"I just didn't know you were dating. He's not new, by the way, he plays basketball."

"Oh. I'm not really dating. Well, I mean, like this is my first date since... you know." Brilliant, Em.

"Yeah. It's okay. It's cool," Tyler says. He manages to make it sound convincing but I've known him long enough to recognize the truth. If Tyler takes the time to mention something and tell you that it's cool, it's not.

"Ty, I'm sorry. I kinda wish she hadn't told you. I bet this is weird." I mean, it's weird for me.

Tyler's hand stops mid x. He gives me that caught-with-your-hand-in-the-cookies stare. "You wouldn't have told me at all?" he asks.

Oops. Never date your friends, y'all. That's my advice. "Well eventually... like if I needed to... this is just a coffee date."

"Emma, we are friends. It's cool. I want you to tell me these things. Maybe it's better this way." He returns to his math.

Apparently my life has become algebra. Too many stupid variables. If Tyler is T and we've dated at least four times then T+E>4. Then Alex, A, enters the equation. How would you mathematically represent that A and E would like to reach 1?

This is crazy. Tyler is right, you can't solve this type of problem without more information.

Chapter 7

NO BIG DEAL. Friends trump infatuations, no matter what the circumstance. Bella is numero uno, no matter how blue Alex's eyes are. No matter how sexy Alex is.

No-no-no. Stop thinking like this Emma, get it together. Bella is your best friend in the world and you will absolutely be at her field hockey game.

I'm in front of the school, waiting to meet with Alex for our date that is too good to be true. I'm doing this nervous habit thing of mine where I stand on the balls of my feet and basically bounce. I'm sure it's great for my calves, but it kind of makes me look like an idiot.

The problem is I can't stop. I'm climbing the world's largest roller coaster from the front cart and it's cloudy. Is there more climbing or am I headed for the plunging downward fall? I guess that depends on whether or not Mr. Alex Slater is the kind of guy who can handle being turned down.

I watch as the students file out of the big, ugly, dirt colored, stucco building. They effortlessly flock to their groups. The group of gamers all produce pocket systems and start thumbing buttons. The group of cheerleaders screech at something. The group of band kids all lugging black plastic cases start heading toward the coffee shop. Then Alex exits with a kid bouncing a basketball.

Have you ever had one of those moments, like in movies, where the world seems to slow down to incredibly slow motion? Like everything slows as Alex rubs the top of his very short black hair with his free hand?

Me neither.

I'm wishing for one though because too soon Alex is standing right in front of me, smiling that heart stopping smile and I still haven't figured out where my voice has run off to. "Emma, are you ready to grab some coffee and teach me a thing or two about Eurasia?" Alex asks.

Here goes nothing. "Actually, something has come up," I blurt. "See, my best friend, Bella Norte, has field hockey tonight. I completely forgot that I promised her I would be at the game. Bella kind of relies on me to be at her games and I am like always there." Have I mentioned I have a tendency to blither when I'm nervous? "So I really have to go to her game. I hope you'll be willing to reschedule because I'd really like to get coffee with you--"

"Why don't I just go with you to the game? I'm into sports," Alex offers. He shrugs his shoulders. "It's not a big deal." Then he does it. He hits me with the absolutely perfect crooked heart-melting smile.

I can't stop the giggle that bubbles up and out of my mouth. "Really?" I ask.

"Really. Shall we go?" Alex turns and heads back toward the

direction of the school.

Does this guy get any more perfect?

It is an absolutely gorgeous day for field hockey. It's not too hot out, owing to the fact that it's late in the year here in Phoenix. The sun is shining, there's a light breeze, and-- oh who am I kidding? It could be raining or miraculously snowing in this hell-hole of a city and I'd still be calling the day perfect. I'm on a date with Alex Slater!

I guiltily admit I spent the entire first period of Bella's game worrying about things that are in no way related to the game of field hockey. I don't think I ever fully focused on the yellow ball rolling up and down the field. I was more worried about where my hands were, where Alex was sitting in proximity to me (did his leg just brush mine?), and whether my breath smelled like lunch.

At the start of the second period, however, my attention is diverted back to the game. The referee blows his whistle, points at Bella, and then lifts his own leg and indicates his foot. Now I'll be honest, I did not completely see the play. But I'm a loyal friend to the end. There was nothing for me to do but abandon my cold metal bleacher and compliment his eyesight. "Are you kidding me, ref? That was clearly hit to her foot on purpose. Are we just letting people draw penalties now? Come on!" I shout.

I sit back down after the opposing team takes, and misses, their penalty shot for the foot call. But now I'm all worked up. My face is red and I'm finally taking in the game.

"You know a lot about this sport?" Alex asks.

"I guess. Bella was on the team last year, I had to do a lot of studying at first."

"You watch any other sports?"

"Not unless I really have to." Then I remember Tyler mentioning something about basketball or football. Whichever one it is, this guy is probably a jock. I quickly think of a cover and peel my eyes from the field to smile at Alex. "I mean I'm sure I'd like more of them but I think I need a reason to learn about it. I'm not really a jump into a random sport kind of girl." Was that better?

Alex nods and I let out the breath I'm holding. "I'm a basketball player myself. Do you play any sports?"

"Not a one. I'm pretty uncoordinated."

"Maybe you can come watch a basketball game sometime," Alex offers. "It could be fun. You could bring Bella along."

"I'd like that." I should explain that mentally I'm doing backflips, which I can't do in real life, across the entire field right now. Hockey game be damned, I'm a happy girl. Alex just invited me on what would technically be a second date and we're not even done with the first one. I turn back to the game so Alex won't see the smile that is so big it makes my eyes squinty. There's got to be some mystery, right?

A bit more of the game passes. Bella scored, forcing Alex and I both to cheer like maniacs. Alex also moved his left leg until it was flush up against my right one and I'm pretty sure it was intentional. This leads me to think I absolutely have to tell someone about this date. I fish my phone out of my pocket. I wish I could text Bella, but she's clearly busy right now.

Tyler? That is probably the most messed up thought I could have. Where did that come from? Who in the world considers texting their ex-boyfriend about their date?

Of course Tyler did just tell me that I can tell him these things.

44

Didn't he even sound hurt when he thought I wouldn't have told him about Alex at all? He certainly looked hurt with that little bad puppy pout on his face.

I glance down at my phone screen. Tyler's face is frozen in a hurt expression, taking up the entire screen. I suck in air and drop the phone. It clangs loudly on the bleachers. Alex and I reach for it at the same time and bonk heads. His noggin is seriously tough; I have to back off to rub my bruised forehead.

Alex retrieves the phone. He flips it right side up and tries to hand it back to me. Tyler's face is still glowing back at us. Dear God, what is wrong with me?

There's silence. Alex offers me a smile and turns his attention back to the field. I hit a button to turn off the screen and hide the offending electronic in my pockct. If I was big on swear words I'd drop one now that would make a sailor blush, let me tell you.

"Who was that guy on your screensaver?" Alex asks. His eyes are still locked on the field.

Crap. "My friend, Tyler." Friend. Friend. Did you hear that choice of words Mr. Slater?

"Yeah? He kind of looks familiar. Does he play a sport?"

"No." I resist the urge to laugh at the thought. "He plays drums."

"Is he like a relative or something?"

"Um, no. He's not really my screen saver. It's just I was…" c'mon Emma, think of a reasonable lie, "…showing his picture to Bella earlier."

"Oh yeah? She doesn't already know him?"

"No, she does." Think girl, think. "He just… um… got a haircut." I physically roll my eyes and toss my head up toward the sky. That was lame.

"Oh."

45

Alright so he's probably not buying it. But what the heck is up with my phone? I push the little button on the top of the screen and it comes back to life. There he is. Still. Only... no, it's probably nothing. It's just, he kind of looks hotter than I remembered. Like, have his eyes always been so captivating?

Nope, this is not a productive line of thinking at all. I quickly hit the home button and safely bring my phone back to the thumbnails for my apps. Before it can do any more thinking of its own I hold the button until the screen goes black.

Technology may very well be ruining my social life.

Chapter 8

"**EARTH TO EMMA,**" Mom calls.

I bring my attention around to her face. If I had to guess by her tone of voice, I'd say it was not the first time she tried to get me to look up from the table. I offer her a smile. "Sorry, what did you say?"

Mom is bustling around the kitchen making dinner. She is still in the black pants and white button up blouse from the suit she wears when she is doing judgy type paperwork stuff. It's different than the slightly more comfortable clothes she wears under her robe on days when she is hearing cases. She has kicked off the heels, so her bare feet are padding around by the stove. I wonder if she ever worries about dropping boiling water on them. She looks over her shoulder at me, seated at the dining table. Her hair has been flipped up in some kind of comb and only a few curly strands ring her face. She kind of frowns at me. "Emma Jean, you need to pay attention. What is going on in that head of yours?" she asks.

I give her the standard teen angst answer, "Nothing."

Her frown deepens until the little wrinkles at the corners of her eyes show up. "Okay, you don't want to talk. I get it." She turns back to the stove. "But if you change your mind, you know where I am."

"I know." My eyes refocus on the table. I probably look like I'm studying the grain of the oak, but I'm totally not. It's just safer to stare at an inanimate object when you're spacing out, you know? I wouldn't want someone to think I'm staring at them. I'm thinking about my disaster of a date, if you can still call it that, yesterday. It's Saturday night. I've lost a whole relaxing Saturday to this already.

Bella says it's nothing to worry about. "Why would someone like Alex Slater be bothered by normal Tyler Garfield?" she asked me when we were discussing the little phone incident on the bleachers.

"I don't know, but he seemed like it bothered him." Didn't he?

"You said Tyler looked familiar to him. Maybe what bothered him is thinking he recognized the face but not being able to place the name. That always bugs me."

Honestly, Bella had a point. She's pretty brilliant. But I am still worried. Main reason? Alex hasn't called.

"Emma, can you clear that junk and set the table for dinner? We need salad plates." Mom smiles over her shoulder. I notice the brown eyes, which I inherited but somehow look much classier on Mom, still look concerned. Our table has exactly three items on it right now. One of those, the napkin holder, always stays on the table. Only someone as organized and practical as my Mom would call the projection remote and a phone "junk."

I have to wipe that concern off Mom's face, so I stand up and get to work. The phone I drop onto the charging pad, the remote I slip into my pocket. I'll be walking by the family room later, why make an extra trip now? Then I get to work setting out three place settings.

Mindless work, this table setting. Frees my mind up to waltz back to the subject of my date. What was his actual reaction when the phone image showed? I try to bring it back to my head. Alex grabbed my phone, but it flipped when he handed it to me. Did it flip or did he flip it? Was he wondering what I was doing on my phone during our date? That can't be good. Maybe he doesn't trust me. Maybe--

"Emma, what are you doing?" Dad emerges into the doorway that separates the kitchen from the family room. Dad dyes the hair on his head back to its original brown, I'm pretty sure. But he can't keep the gray out of his beard and mustache. It makes him look tired. Also, the hair on his head is sticking up a little on one side. This is a sure sign he's stressed, because he tugs it upward when he's really working on a difficult problem.

"Setting the table," I answer. Seriously, what did he think I was doing?

"With the projection screen. What are you doing with that?" Dad says.

"Nothing." What is he talking about? I lean away from the table, trying to see around Dad. "I'm not even in there, Dad."

"I was replaying my test subject samples for something important and you interrupted with some juvenile escapade. It's hardly appropriate..."

Yeah, see, I stopped listening. I didn't interrupt his work. I'm not that dumb. I walk past Dad into the family room. The furniture in this room is all pointed toward the giant projection screen. Since Dad helped design it, it's one of the best models. The projector is behind the wall, so it doesn't take up space in the ceiling or anything like some older models. It's basically flat and you can see it from anywhere in the room. Which means I can see the full screen image of Alex, hand on my cell phone, from last night.

"What the hell?" It slips out.

"Emma Jean, watch your mouth!" Mom yells from the kitchen.

"Why is it frozen on this?" I ask Dad. Evidently he's followed me into the room. "Why is it showing this at all?" I walk up to the side of the screen. I'd like to smack my hand on it, clear up whatever stupid connection this thing thinks it has, but I don't know where to hit it.

"It's still picking up on you, Emma. But it's frozen. You must be still thinking about whatever this is, otherwise it would be black. Can you please just hand over the controls?"

"I don't have control. I didn't... oh wait." I fish the remote out of my pocket and offer it to Dad. "Is it because of this? It was on the table."

Dad crosses the room and takes the remote from me. As soon as I drop my hand to my side the screen goes black. Only a little blue light in the bottom right corner is there to indicate the unit is still on and ready to receive data.

"Emma, did you send that video?" Dad asks. His voice is lower. I don't think he's angry anymore, suddenly he sounds concerned.

"No." I swallow with an audible gulp. It was a whole video? How embarrassing.

"What do you mean, no? How is that possible?" Mom's tall lanky frame fills the doorway. "What is going on here?" she asks. Her eyes flit back and forth between me and Dad like a field hockey goalie trying to figure out which one of us will shoot first.

"Emma has been having some troubles with her chip," Dad answers.

"Wait, you said it couldn't be my chip," I challenge.

"Fine, Emma has been sending things accidentally with her chip."

"For how long?" Mom asks.

"A few days, Mom." This is new ground. Never in my entire 16 years have I taken an issue to Dad before Mom. I hope she's not offended.

"She came to me wondering if it could be her chip. I didn't think it was." Dad sinks into his recliner and rubs his chin. "Hannah, it's possible I was mistaken." He fixes Mom with a serious expression. "We need to take her to Carl. He will want to run some tests."

"Is that necessary?" Mom asks.

Yeah, is that necessary? I thought we said it was nothing.

"It can't hurt. Maybe we just need someone to look into it. That video was blurry, like a memory, but Emma had the remote in her pocket and obviously didn't intend to send it. Carl would have the equipment to run more tests than I do. I'll call him myself after dinner."

"Could it just be the technology?" I ask. "Like the screen is acting up?"

"Wasn't your phone involved last time?" Dad asks.

Oh yeah, I forgot about that. "I guess."

"No, the only common factor appears to be you. I'll call Carl." Dad rises and claps his hands. "He'll be able to figure this all out and then everything will return to normal." He cups my shoulder and smiles down at me. "Let's eat, I'm starving."

Dad leaves for the kitchen. I look over at Mom. She is not smiling. I offer her a shrug. "It'll be fine. He knows this stuff, Ma."

I hope.

Chapter 9

"CAN I BE excused?" I haven't really been into the whole eating-dinner-with-the-family thing tonight. After the remote control debacle, I just want to get upstairs and call Bella. I figure since Dad just slipped away from the table, I should be allowed to as well.

Mom gives me that awkward side smile, the one that means she is feeling sorry for me. I'd tell her I don't want her pity, but her pity may work in my favor right now. I drop my chin a little lower, really laying it on thick.

"Of course you can. I'll take care of the clean up."

She's laying on the guilt, I think. She made dinner, she shouldn't have to clean it up. But I really want to call Bells. So I leave. I'm kind of stomping down the hallway, a fact I probably would never have noticed if Dad's office door had not had that line of light marking the floor. It's open. That means I can make too much noise and completely disturb whatever he is doing. My feet turn to pillows as I take each step slowly.

"...it's not like the first time," Dad sounds irritated at whoever he is talking to. He has that short, clipped, angry tone he usually reserves for me. I admit it, I'm curious. I pause, one foot in front of the other. This way I can give the appearance of still making slow progress toward my room if someone were to come in.

"Yes," he says. There's a few moments of silence before I hear Dad's frustrated, you're-not-understanding-me sigh followed by a pointed "yes". The air in the hallways starts to get stale as it sits for several seconds. Finally, he gives the same reply a third time, audibly losing his patience.

Hearing only one side of a phone conversation is basically useless. I put the weight on my right foot, ready to start moving again.

"Dammit, Carl. You're not understanding. This is already recorded, it would be a second instance."

Whoa, Carl? Isn't that the guy at work Dad said he had to call? My cheeks are turning warm, like someone poured hot water over my head. Are they talking about me? Technically, if Dad told this guy about the coffee shop instance, this would be a second occurrence. I swallow what feels like a jawbreaker in my throat and lean a little closer to the door.

"I'm sure. Listen, we just need to run some tests. I want to see what we are dealing with."

Dad has adopted a slightly calmer voice now. If he deals with Carl like he deals with me this tells me that Carl has started to cave. Dad is using the 'I'm-on-your-side' voice now. If it works and Carl agrees with him, Dad will thank him. If it doesn't--

"Because it needs to be done!"

--then Dad will adopt that angry because-I-said-so voice. The one that even made me flinch in the hallway when it wasn't directed at me.

That's the last resort. That will work. I have never seen anyone stand up to Dad when he gets like that. Even I'm ready to cave, whatever we were talking about. Plus, I'm kind of on Dad's side here. Don't I want some testing done too? Don't I want to know what is going on? C'mon Carl, help a girl out.

"Thank you, that's all I was asking."

Sounds like Carl agreed. I start moving toward my room again, feeling triumphant. It's not until my hand closes on the handle that I wonder what Carl's objection was.

Is there something about this testing Dad is not telling me?

Chapter 10

ONE TIME I had to go to school the day before my family went to Disneyland. I spent the entire day just watching the clock move. It was like someone had put the little mechanical hands in molasses, they didn't move much at all. Today is worse. Today I know I'm visiting with Dad's friend, Carl... something. Carl is supposed to tell me whether my chip is malfunctioning. Carl is supposed to tell me what we can do about it. I think I'd be less nervous if you told me I was scheduled to walk on a tightrope across the Grand Canyon today.

"So Emma, I hear you made it to the game without incident," Tyler says. He drops into the chair next to me. Tyler looks good today. Oh man, did I really just think that? I can't really control my own thoughts about it. It's like a reflex. He's not hot in the way Alex is. He's more... adorable. Maybe it's the soft brown hair or the intoxicating brown eyes. Tyler reminds me of a teddy bear, comforting and completely charming.

"Morning, Ty. Yeah, I made it," I answer.

"Alex went along, I hear. That's a great solution, whose idea was that?"

I look at him with what I can only imagine is shock. He is digging through his backpack, not looking in my direction at all. "Um, yeah. It was kind of his idea, I guess." How does he know all this? "Ty, did you talk to Bella or something?"

"Well yeah, but that's not where I got this information. Alex and I have a class together."

Alex and Tyler have a... and they talked about... oh man, this just got weird again. "What, um, what else did you two talk about?"

"Not much." He evidently finds what he was looking for in his backpack, producing a notebook that he slams down onto the table. He offers me a shy smile. "I've actually never had a conversation with him before. He sat next to me today and introduced himself. He said you told him we were friends. Any friend of yours is a friend of his, apparently."

"Oh." The unasked question burns my mouth like coffee that's too hot. But I just won't let myself spit it out. I puff out my cheeks, like that will give the idea a place to roost.

"He seems like a nice guy, Ems."

"Isn't this weird, talking about a guy I went on a date with?" I ask. Honestly I'm glad that's the question that tumbled out. When I opened my mouth I was a little worried it was going to be the picture question I'm restraining.

"No." The bell rings. Tyler turns his notebook to a blank page and writes the date at the top. Seeing that I'm not going to get a better answer than that, I echo the movement. I feel Tyler's warm hand tap me on my upper thigh through my black jeans. He points to his notebook when I look at him. "It was only weird when he asked about my haircut."

Tyler has scribbled this across the top of the clean sheet of paper.

"Oh, um, I can explain that," I whisper.

"Later." He smiles.

Good, that will give me time to come up with that explanation.

We learn something new and complicated in class today. That means all my energy and focus goes into the skill instead of into creating a plausible reason for telling Alex that Tyler got a haircut he never got. Why was I even talking about Tyler on my date, anyway? Before I have time to think about it, the teacher announces group work time.

"Partners?" Ty offers. "I totally get this stuff."

"Yeah, of course."

"Good. So you were saying, about the haircut?" Tyler flips open his textbook and starts leafing through pages.

"Oh yeah, a picture of you was up on my phone. I was trying to figure out how to explain why it was there. I just kind of lied. I told Alex it was because you had just gotten a haircut." That was entirely more truth than I had imagined giving. The problem with me is I value truth. Even embarrassing truth.

Tyler's hands stop flipping pages. He squints at me. "A picture of me was on your phone? Should I ask why?"

"Yeah, I don't really know. Something is up with me. Dad thinks it might be my chip. It's sort of sending memories up whenever it wants." Truth again. Damn.

Now I have his full attention. He spins his chair toward me. "What? Seriously? Emma, that's a little scary. What are you doing about it?"

"I'm seeing Dad's friend Carl something today. He's supposed to run some diagnostic tests or whatever."

"Carl Simons? He's awesome."

"Yeah, I guess. Do you know him?"

"He's in the news like all the time. He's super famous. Kind of like..."

He doesn't finish the sentence. He doesn't have to. I'm perfectly aware that Tyler kind of hero crushes on my father. It's weird, but I've accepted it.

"At least I'm seeing the best, right?" I shrug. "Alright, let's get back to math."

"Yeah, of course. We'll both try number one and then compare answers," Tyler offers.

Right, math. I guess now that I'm thinking about chips, brain scans, and tight ropes, algebra is a stroll on the beach.

Chapter 11

DOWNTOWN PHOENIX IS a sea of building, people, and concrete. There is no real nature anywhere you look. It's a bustling cityscape that breathes stress. Just being nearby makes my heartbeat pick up.

Dad's building is located in the heart of downtown, right off of Central Avenue. Years of practice maneuvering through this area have Dad at ease behind the wheel. Even when another car swerves in front of us and makes me gasp, Dad just taps the brakes and slows down.

He flashes his badge at the security booth as we approach the parking lot. It earns him a head nod and a hearty, "Good morning, Mr. Johnson," from the guy in the booth.

The building is not the tallest on the street, but it shares a parking lot with one monstrosity that sure is. Both buildings alternate a row of full windows, which appear black from this angle, with a copper gone wrong that appears too orange. The result is a pair of sad tigers standing sentry over the shared parking lot.

We enter into the lobby and get blasted with heat. It's maybe fifty degrees outside, being what we call winter in Phoenix. It's not really cold, but it sure feels like it after you spent all summer in weather that never dipped below one hundred. That makes this our jacket weather. Turn on the heat in your nature killer of a building weather.

"Good morning, Mr. Johnson," a man dressed in a blue security uniform calls out from behind a desk. "Could you please sign and scan in your guest?"

"She's not my guest today, Tom. I'm off the clock. We're here to see Carl."

"Alright, sign in both of you then." He waits for Dad to scribble in the log book and then scans both our chips with a wand. "Have a nice meeting."

The last comment is called as we step away from the counter toward the bay of steel elevators to wait for a trip up to the seventh floor. I'm doing that thing again. The one where I bounce on the balls of my feet. Mom would place her tiny little hand on my shoulder to silently stop me from doing it if she were here. She had a court case this afternoon. Dad claimed it was nothing we couldn't handle together. He never notices the bounce.

Carl Simons turns out to be younger than I expected, which is to say younger than my Dad. Skinny, dark hair and eyes, dapper in that older man kind of way. No sign that the stress of the job is graying anything on his handsome face. "You must be Emma," he says, offering me his hand. "I'd say you're a little nervous."

"A little," I say. My smile is fake. I wonder if he can tell that too.

"Well don't be. We're not going to do anything weird or painful today. Most of what I do is on a computer screen. Why don't you follow me back and we'll get started?"

I don't have time to protest because Carl's long legs are off down the hall. I have to jog to keep up with his speed, and I'm pretty tall. We enter into a room with one large old-fashioned computer monitor and a skinny black computer tower sitting on an otherwise empty glass topped desk. There are two chairs. One beside the desk and the other in front of it. "Where's Dad supposed to sit?" I ask.

"In the lobby," Carl answers, dropping himself into the chair facing the screen.

What have I gotten myself into?

Chapter 12

"**ALRIGHT, I HEAR** you've been having trouble with your chip. I'm going to run a few simple diagnostic tests today and then I'll need to do a log file dump before you leave which will give me even more detail that I may or may not need. I'll look through all of that and get back to you with the results as soon as I can." Carl explains all this while the sound of his fingers clicking keys on the keyboard echoes throughout the room.

I cannot see the screen from my seat beside it to know what he's doing. Of course even if I could see it there's no guarantee I'd understand it. Kind of like I don't understand much of what he just said. Except test. I got that word.

The computer Carl is sitting in front of looks a lot like the one in my Dad's office at home. It's older and boxier than the models you can buy now. There's a bunch of wires coming out of the back of the old tower, reaching for the wall and tethering the machine to this location. There must be something unique about this old school machine. Otherwise, why would a bunch of technology gurus at the best facility in the country have them? Can't they afford something newer?

Carl's fingers stop typing and he smiles at me. "Emma, I'm going to show you three cards. Pay attention." Carl produces an Ace of Diamonds, a Queen of Hearts, and a red Joker from his vest pocket. "Got them?" he asks.

"Yes. What does that--"

"Excellent." He cuts me off and slides the cards back into the pocket. "Now I want you to call up a memory for me. Any memory. In fact, the further back the memory is the better it is for me. Can you do that?"

"Well yes, but--"

"Good." This is an annoying habit, he could let me finish a sentence. "Go ahead and tap the connection plate when you are ready."

Thankfully he points to the little black rectangle sitting beside the old-fashioned computer tower when he says this. I'm relatively certain I did not know that this little rectangle, connected by some long wire to the computer, is the same kind of plate I've used and seen before. I concentrate on a memory from third grade and tap the plate.

I cannot see the screen but the memory is clear in my head. I close my eyes to enjoy it. We are in my third grade classroom. Mrs. May had set up the desks to promote grouping. She had randomly assigned two girls and two boys to each group. I was assigned the table with a purple basket at the center.

"Hi, I'm Emma," I tell the table. "I believe in unicorns." Alright, I was a dork. Let's please remember I was also like eight.

"I'm Annabella but my friends call me Bella. I totally love unicorns. We should be friends." *She flashes me a mouth full of crooked baby teeth. Her scraggly blonde almost-curls pop out of her ponytail. This is someone I could get along with.*

"Best friends," I say.

"I'm Tyler and I believe in..." eight year old Tyler rips off the loudest most disgusting fart I've ever heard. The other little boy laughs and they high five.

"You better call me Annabella," Bella says. Then she leans into me like we're sharing our first delicious piece of secret pie. "He is gross."

The memory fades. I pop my eyes open and smile. This time it's genuine. I just love those two.

"Excellent. Thank you. Now can you show me what cards I showed you earlier? In order?" Carl asks.

Oh crap. I close my eyes and try to remember. Ace of something. Diamonds, maybe. Here's the cool thing about your brain. Sometimes you actually remember more than you think you do. I picture the Ace of Diamonds and tap the connection plate again.

Ace of Diamonds. Queen of Hearts. Joker.

"What color was that joker, Emma?" He tilts the screen in my direction so I can see the image is appearing without color. Oh, um... black. Maybe?

Black Joker.

The screen colors in. "Emma, the joker was red." Carl produces

64

the three cards from his vest pocket again, flashing it toward me to prove it. The Joker on screen changes color before I move my wrist away and break the connection. This must be an old NFC chip, its range is not very far.

"Good job, Emma." Carl moves the screen back toward him before he starts clicking away at the keyboard again. The actual act of typing on a keyboard must help him think, it's not really a necessary step anymore. I mean, obviously, if you can think it you can type it. "Alright Emma, now we are going to try interruption. I am going to run a memory of my own. You are going to try and break into it using any memory you want. Stronger memories are probably better. You shouldn't be able to break in, so don't worry if you can't. I do want you to try your best though."

"Okay." I guess. Except I broke in on Dad's video memory without even trying. I wasn't supposed to be capable of that? That's news. My stomach is flipping out right now as I try to think of a memory strong enough. I finally settle on the field hockey game with Alex. That was strong enough for Dad.

I picture Tyler's image showing up on my phone. Alex reaching for it. That heart stopping moment, watching Alex's fingers getting close.

I tap the connection plate before the memory progresses much further.

"Try harder, Emma. My memory is still showing."

Okay, okay. I keep my hand on the connection plate. Maybe I need a stronger memory. Maybe the memory of the first time I kissed someone. I blush just thinking about showing this to one of Dad's coworkers. But I already thought it, can't stop it now.

I'm sitting on the top row of bleachers, waiting for Bella after her game. There are little sprinkles of rain making everything look shiny. Tyler is sitting next to me, close enough to make me aware of his body heat. He slips his arm around my shoulders and leans toward me. My heart is slamming into my ribcage, trying to get loose. When his lips connect with mine, I lose all sensation. I can't feel the rain, I can't feel my rapid heart, I can't feel the cold metal bleacher. I just feel Tyler. His lips, his arm heavy on my shoulder, his tongue pushing my lips apart.

"Interesting." Carl's voice snaps me back to reality.

I open my eyes and blush a deep crimson, I'm sure. What did he see? "What's interesting? Did it break through?"

Carl offers me a smile. "Don't worry about it at all." Click-click-clickity-click on the keyboard. "Alright, earlier I asked you to recall three cards. You remembered one of them incorrectly. Show me the mistake."

Tap the connection plate and go.

Black Joker that blooms into a Red Joker.

"Good. Alright, one more and then we'll do that dump I told you about. This is the hardest one yet. I need you to think of one thing while trying to hold a projection of something else for me. It should be possible for you to have an image up, command it to freeze, and let your mind wander. Can you try that for me? Show me a sunset. Don't let me see what you are remembering after that," Carl says.

Here goes nothing. Tap and hold.

A sunset, as requested. Now, freeze that image.

Now let my mind wander. Okay, um, well Alex I guess. Alex's blue eyes and little I'm-really-trying-to-pay-attention forward glance but smiling at me. Alex taking nice, organized notes. Bella does that too. Actually so does Tyler. Maybe I'm the weird one. I need to take nicer notes. I wonder if one of them will teach me to do that.

"Alright, Emma. I have everything I need," Carl says. I quickly move my hand away from the connection plate. I wonder if the sunset stayed frozen. "I need you to think about the phrase 'log file dump' and tap the plate again," says Carl.

"I don't know what that means."

"That's alright, your chip does. It's a command it will understand." Carl turns the monitor toward me. "Just watch what it does when you give that command. 'Log file dump.' Got it?"

I lay my hand on the connection thing again, my eyes fixed on the screen.

Log file dump.

The black screen is suddenly alive with green digits. They are moving up the screen like a million tiny bugs on attack, scrolling so fast I cannot hope to read them. I'm careful to keep my wrist in place. Who knew all this was on there? "What is all that?" I ask.

"Everything your chip has sent or received. Do you remember the date stamp of the last time your chip malfunctioned?"

"Date stamp?"

"Date and time," Carl modifies.

"Oh." The screen is still rolling digits. Carl pushes back away from the desk, letting the file dump collect everything. When was the last... oh, right. Alex. "It messed up during a field hockey game on Friday. The game started around 4. It was during the third period that it messed up."

"So, around 5 at night on Friday?"

"I suppose so."

"That's helpful, Emma. Thanks."

The screen has stopped moving. I scan my eyes down it, trying to see what my chip is revealing about me. It's total gibberish. Great, my chip and I don't even speak the same language. Carl turns the screen back toward him.

"This is great, a lot of data here." He stands up. "Alright Emma, I have everything I need. Let's get you back to your Dad so I can dive into all this."

The walk back to the lobby is silent. I have no idea what memories of mine this guy saw. Did he see my kiss? How embarrassing is that? Did I pass the tests or fail miserably? I wish he'd give me something.

"How'd it go?" Dad practically jumps from his chair to greet us. Judging by his body language, feet and hips pointed away from me, he's talking to Carl. I stay stoic as a statue, resisting the urge to roll my eyes.

"She did well. I have a lot to analyze," Carl answers.

"Did you test her interruption skills?"

"Of course I did. I ran a full diagnostic, Steve. I'll let you know." Carl sounds a bit irritated.

"Do you have any preliminary thoughts?"

Carl is silent for a second, holding Dad's gaze. This guy has guts. My Dad has a stare that will make you squirm. He should interrogate prisoners of war or something with that stare. But Carl meets it. "I'll let you know," Carl repeats.

It's more guts than I was expecting, given what happened on the phone. I look to Dad, waiting for the stern tone again.

"Fine," Dad answers.

Fine? You're letting him win this one? I'm filled with a new appreciation for Carl.

Dad looks down, finally acknowledging me. "You ready to go home, then?"

"Yup." Don't ask me about it, Dad. I wouldn't know anything anyway. I mean, seriously, I don't. I almost wish I knew more so I could meet that interrogative stare head on and pull a Carl, shutting down Dad's questions. "Dad, why didn't you tell me it's not supposed to be possible to interrupt a projection?" I ask as the elevator doors close behind us.

"You didn't need to know that. I didn't want to worry you."

"But that was the reason you agreed something might be wrong, right?" I couldn't convince him in his office. It wasn't until I was able to override something he was projecting that he agreed to have my chip checked.

"Yes."

"What exactly could be wrong with it, Dad? What will they do if it's busted?"

Dad gives me an I-don't-want-to-talk-about-this look. "I don't know. It's never happened before."

Maybe they'll put me in a history book, then. "But they can fix it, right?"

"I hope so."

I don't say anything else all the way home. Because I can't. Because the great Steve Johnson just had to use the word 'hope' when talking about his technology. Steve Johnson does not 'hope.' Steve

Johnson 'does' or 'doesn't.' I'm not sure what it means for me that he is left with only hope.

Chapter 13

—▪—▪——▪———▪—▪——▪———▪—▪——▪———▪—▪——▪———▪—▪—

IT'S A KNOWN fact that you always sit in the same row during the History lecture. Unless she moves you or you are super late. I've been a victim of both. You don't have to be in the same seat, but you don't row jump without reason. I prefer the seat in the top row on the left hand side of the aisle. Yes, it's because that's the easiest seat to slip into when you are late. I'm not late today. It's 7:58, I checked. But guess who is sitting in the seat directly next to the one I take? My heart is doing this weird fluttery thing when I stop next to him. "Hi Alex."

He turns his head toward me and the whole room lights up with that smile. "Hey Emma. How have you been?"

I drop into the seat next to him. "Good. How about you?" It comes off as flippant, casual. It's totally not. I'm a Mexican jumping bean inside.

"Good. I believe you owe me a coffee. I checked and there is no field hockey game today. Would you like to grab coffee with me after school?"

Do fish live in water? "Yeah, I could do that." Ohmygod.

Mrs. Straightier starts class promptly at 8 with a little throat-clearing and a slide show. I slip my notebook, pen, and phone onto the little desk I've flipped up. I have a text from Bella. "Marcus is sitting NEXT TO ME. OMG what do I do?"

The giggle slips out even though I try to hide it. Alex glances questioningly at me. I point to my phone. He shakes his head, but he's still smiling. It's good I can make him laugh, right? Reply.

"Um, talk to him?"

"You make it sound so easy." Bella's reply is instant. This girl has a bad crush if she's willing to be texting during class. Poor thing. Reply

"He's just a person, Bells. Pretend he's Ty."

I hold the phone a bit longer in case a reply comes through. It doesn't. I try to crane my neck and see around the rows between us. Bella will be parked in the second row from the front. That means there are a lot of Sophomores crammed into the giant classroom between us. I can see her blonde hair, I think, but it looks like she's facing forward.

"Who are you looking for?" Alex asks in his I'm-paying-attention whisper voice.

"Bella. She was texting me."

"I'm taller than you. Sit back, I'll look. Where does she sit?"

"Second row." I sit back. "See if she's, like, talking to someone."

Alex gives me a strange look. "If I find her it'll be the back of her head."

"Yeah, I know." I figure Alex will give up on his offer. He doesn't. He leans forward in his chair until he's practically sticking his nose in the curls of the girl in front of him. He stands on his tiptoes pulling his adorable butt up out of the chair. He stays frozen like that, moving his head around left and right.

When he drops back into the chair I fix my eyes on Straightier to keep us from getting caught with all these acts of blatant inattention. "I found her. She's sitting on the right hand aisle so the only person next to her is Marcus. She's facing forward, I'm pretty sure. He kept turning his head toward her though, so maybe they're talking. Does that help?" Alex rushes his explanation and then turns his eyes back toward the front as well.

"You're awesome, thanks." Immediately, my face gets hot. Little beads of sweat form on my forehead, I can feel them. I just said he was awesome. I should've said "that's awesome" or just "thanks." I'm so embarrassing sometimes.

Knowing Bella is on the opposite side of the aisle, I lean away from Alex and look that way. Of course there is still a long downward distance to look, but I can see her from here. I watch for a few minutes. Sure enough, she keeps turning her head slightly right and then snapping it back to the left. Her hair is flouncing about every time she does it. They *are* talking. Point-Bella.

I sit back in my chair and glance at my watch. 8:20. Today is going to be one of those days when time just crawls by at a snail's pace again. I look at Alex. It's his fault. I will be waiting on this coffee shop date all day. After all, with the disaster date that collided with my technology problem, I thought I was doomed. I can't believe how lucky I am. Alex must have bought the whole haircut story after all.

But what should I do about the technology? I can't let another picture pop up or another coffee shop debacle happen. Maybe I shouldn't go on this date until I hear from Carl and know what I'm dealing with.

"Hey Alex," I whisper.

He turns his head a little toward me, enough so I can see one blue eye. "Hey what?"

"I've been waiting for a call from my doctor, so I may have to rush off today after school. I'll meet you out front and let you know, okay?" It's not exactly a lie. It's the best I can do, I can't break another date with him. I don't want to. Maybe Carl will call and leave a message saying I'm all cured by the magic of technology and his old school keyboard.

"That's cool. I hope you can come."

"Me too." Seriously.

Chapter 14

Snail paced History followed by seven other incredibly slow and boring class periods later I'm sitting in the coffee shop while Alex picks up our coffees. Bella, via text messages, managed to convince me that I should show up. Any little "issue" I may be experiencing sounds like something that can be solved by avoiding technology. According to Bells the solution is to avoid my phone, sit opposite the projector plate in the coffee house (check), and just be attentive to Alex by leaving all technology alone.

Tyler, for his part, mentioned that Alex was excited about the date. Apparently they sat together in class, again, and discussed it. Ty claims they also discussed other things, but it was confirmed this is actually a date. So there's that.

"Alright, here's your mocha." Alex sets the mug that currently looks like it's full past capacity with only whipped cream directly in front of me. He sips from his cup. Whatever he's drinking, it's without the aerosol dairy product.

"You don't like whipped cream?" I ask. Great at date conversation, that's me.

"Not with coffee."

Okay. Officially out of things to talk to smoldering blue eyes about. I decide to play it cool and cute, flirty even. I channel my best rom-com voice. "Did you really need help with the Eurasian Union or was that just a convenient excuse to ask me on a date?"

Alex laughs. "A little of both actually. Do you understand the whole job situation?" Alex pulls his phone out.

My heart flutters. No, no, no. Not technology. I'm supposed to avoid technology. "Um… what are you doing?"

"I'm going to show you the topic." Alex chuckles like I'm trying to be funny. Avoiding technology is not something people will understand. Alex commands a video to start and tips the phone so I can see it too. I keep my hands firmly planted in my lap and watch.

Straightier, during class. The slide behind her says only one word: jobs. There were likely other words there at one point but Alex must not remember them, they've gone fuzzy. "That helped lead to job growth, which of course stimulates the economy because people who make money spend money. That economic growth in the Union continues to make them a profitable nation."

The POV moves to the right. There's me, sitting next to Alex, clicking away on my own phone in my own little world. I look exactly like I remember looking that day in my 'maybe she runs to school' outfit.

The video ends. "See, I have no idea what she was talking about.

Why would the Union of two countries in Europe and Asia lead to more jobs?" Alex asks.

I feel the stress slip out of my tightly knotted shoulders as Alex slips the phone back into the pocket of his jeans. "Three nations," I mumble.

"What?"

"It was three nations. Two of which didn't have much opportunity for jobs in their own countries, they were hurting financially. Merging with Russia allowed them to share a common economic system, which means they could get jobs either dealing with that or take jobs in Russia." I could probably cite him the author I stole that from in my research but the thing about teenagers is we traditionally don't care about that. If he has to write a paper or something, he'll just look it up himself. I'm sure he knows this isn't an original thought I had on my own.

"Alright, I suppose that kind of makes sense. All this is a little useless isn't it? Why do we have to learn about this?"

"I agree." I resist the urge to offer my hand to high-five over this shared ground. "Mergers and declarations of independence have happened countless times since the beginning of time. Why do we have to learn about every single one of them?"

"Maybe she's trying to encourage us to stand up and declare ourselves independent from her line of thinking," Alex offers.

We both break into laughter. As the laughter breaks apart I remember we are in public. Other people just saw me laughing with Alex Slater. Sweet. "So Alex, when is your next basketball game?" I shamelessly lean a little closer to him, putting more of my weight on the little round table between us.

"Thursday after school. Are you gonna make it?"

"I'll try."

"That would be great." He looks like he means it; his whole face lights up.

A buzzing noise starts. I look around, trying to figure out where it is coming from. It stops. When it starts again I realize it's probably a phone. "Is your phone on vibrate?" I ask.

Alex pulls it out of his pocket. I pull back in my chair like that poisonous electronic is going to strike out and bite my wrist to reveal some personal memory to Alex. The light on the top is blinking. "Oh, it's my coach. I'm gonna take this," he says, frowning.

"Okay, no problem."

Alex steps outside, phone raised to his ear. I look around the coffee shop. It's fun to know people saw you on a date, especially if you know the people. There's only about ten people in the shop today, not including the baristas in their green aprons behind the counter. I recognize a few toward the projection screen as students at our school, but I certainly don't know their names. Today would've been a cool day to have Tom Martin and Chris White sitting here. Maybe they'd go back to school and tell everyone that I was on a date with Alex Slater. I'm sure they know Alex, he plays sports. Chris knew my name, I recall with a smile. That means they would be perfectly capable of spreading that rumor for me.

The coffee shop door dings as Alex pulls it back open. No sign of the phone, so he must have returned that to the pocket. His hair and shoulders are wet, glistening and dripping as he shakes them off. "Raining out there." He stops behind his seat, hovering.

"Everything okay?"

"Yeah, but I have to go. We were supposed to meet on the field to run before practice, but obviously that's out because of rain. Coach wants us to meet at the gym down on Thunderbird. It's like a mile and a half up the road so I should go back and get my car. I'm sorry. I thought we'd have more time," Alex says.

His eyes are sort of crinkled around the edges and there's a little frown forming. He looks sorry, I decide. But he does not look like I can change his mind. "Yeah, okay. I'll walk back to school with you." I grab my coffee and stand up.

"Great, thanks Emma. Sorry about this."

"Yeah, no problem." I offer him a 'see, I'm cool' smile. Of course what I'm really thinking is how it turns out to be good Chris and Tom were not here today. I don't need the whole school knowing the score is officially Basketball - 1, Emma - 0.

Chapter 15

WE HAVE A really cute little house. It's Arizona-style stucco on the outside, like everyone else's, but inside it's just adorable. When I walk inside after my date I'm standing in the living room. There is a coat rack to my right which my Mother picked out. It's tall and gold and very fancy looking. There's a purple and gold carpet in the living room and the dark furniture looks great sitting on it. It's all arranged so that everyone can face the projection screen on the wall, which is normally what we are all looking at when we are in here. Normally.

Of course today they're both looking at me the second I walk in. Both of them. Together. Perched on the couch, looking like two cats sitting on a fence near the dog pound. Nervous.

"What's going on?" I drop my backpack on the floor and start nervously bouncing on my toes.

"Emma Jean, don't bounce like that. You don't need to be

nervous. Come sit down." Mom pats the couch next to her. "We just wanted to talk to you."

"About what?" I'm already stepping toward the couch. It's instinct. Your mother asks you to sit, you sit. Especially when your mother is a judge.

"Carl called," Dad answers.

That stops me. I'm frozen halfway to the couch, staring at both of my parents. "He did?"

"Yes. Have a seat, please, let's talk about it," Mom pleads.

"You're chip is malfunctioning," Dad says.

"Steve, I asked you to ease into it." Mom is up out of her seat. She meets me where I'm frozen, wraps her arm delicately around my shoulders, and steers me to the furniture.

Clearly this is the routine they plan to fall into today. Dad will be blunt and give answers. Mom will comfort. Good cop, bad cop for parents. I look at Dad. "Tell me what that means."

"It means it's not your fault. Something happened to the chip, somehow. It's doing things it shouldn't be able to do."

"Like interrupt projections." It comes out of my mouth as a question.

"Just like that." Dad nods.

Mom has started rubbing slow circles on my back. "What happens next?" I ask Dad. "Will they just take it out?"

Dad turns his eyes away from me for just a second, exchanging a glance with Mom. That sends my stomach rocketing down to my toes. What was that all about?

"They can't take it out, Em." Dad is speaking in an uncharacteristically quiet voice. "They were designed for lifetime wear. We have never done a single test on what would happen if we remove it now that it has become part of your nervous system."

"Are you kidding me? You're kidding me, right?" I say. "A group of brilliant scientists embedded a chip into a human being without knowing whether it could ever be removed?" Okay I'm sort of yelling at my own father, somewhere my brain has to recognize that as stupid.

"We can take you to a neurologist, honey," Mom says. "There was a neurologist on the original team. He helped to map out the installation and all those things. I'm sure he would be the person to speak with about removing it."

"So it may still be removable?" I'm still looking at Dad.

"Maybe," he answers. "We can hope."

Damn. That word again. Steve Johnson is hoping about his technology. I hang my head. "Is there anything else or can I go to my room?"

"You can go, honey. Do you need anything?" Mom asks.

I just shake my head, no, as I head to my room. I don't think this is something you can solve with warm tea or hot cocoa.

Once I hit my bed, I throw my phone onto my pink speaker dock. I tap the screen, giving it the command to call Bella. Then I stare at my wrist while I listen to it ring through the speakerphone. You're the one causing all this trouble, I think. Somewhere deep in there, wrapped in wires or something, there's a tiny little data chip and it's causing all this.

"Hello my dear," Bella answers.

"Hey."

"Uh-oh. You sound disquieted."

"Does that mean the same as rattled, frustrated, sick, and worried?"

"Sort of. What's up, Ems?"

"Carl called. My chip is malfunctioning." Saying it out loud makes it real. Tears burn behind my eyes. "Even worse, the brilliant team of scientists never tested whether the chip could be removed because it was designed for lifetime wear."

"Okay, what does that mean? Like what's our next step?"

"I have to go see a neurologist."

"That's good, Em. They're brain doctors. I mean, if you work on the human brain for a living, what can't you do? These people are brilliant. They'll be able to take it out. Are you going to have them put a new one in?"

She sounds so confident that it starts to bleed into me. "I don't know, I haven't even thought about that. Do you really think they'll be able to take it out?"

"Oh my goodness, yes. These people go to school for years and years so they can be certified to cut up tiny pieces of your brain without leaving you damaged. Do you think they'll be afraid to cut into your wrist? No. This will be easy-peasy. You'll see."

"Well you're making me feel a little better--"

"That is my job, girl. What else do you need?" She giggles a little. "Can we talk about the date?"

"What date?"

"Did you or did you not just get home from a coffee date with Mr. Alex Slater?"

"Oh yeah, I did." In all the chaos that met me at the door I actually forgot. "It was good, I guess. It got cut a little short because of basketball practice, so we didn't really have time to talk much."

"Oh, that's too bad. I guess that means no see-you-tomorrow kissy face?"

I can't help it. I laugh. Kissy face? She is a goof. "Not this time," I tell her. "He did ask me to come to his basketball game on Thursday.

Actually I think you should come too, if you can."

"I totally can. It'll be fun."

"You're the best, Bells." I mean it too. My heart is feeling like it's pumping at normal speed right now and my teenage brain has gone back where it belongs, to thinking about boys. Everyone needs a friend like this.

"Alright then, I'm going to go finish my homework." She sighs. "Emma, seriously, they'll fix this. You'll see. Don't stress, okay?"

"Yeah, alright. Thanks Bella."

When we hang up the phone, I'm smiling. They can fix this. You can keep your hope, Dad. We got this.

Chapter 16

MARK YOUR CALENDARS, ladies and germs. It's a school day and Emma Jean Johnson is awake at six in the morning. It's Thursday, the day which will require prep and effort. I'm standing in front of my closet bemoaning the fact that everything in there is just not right for a basketball game date. What does one wear when they need to look smoking hot and yet need to look as though it happened by accident? When you need to fit in at a basketball game? Keep in mind that this magical item must also come from my closet. Hopeless, that's what this is.

"Call Bella," I command my phone. From where it sits on the speaker it comes to life and starts dialing.

"Hello?"

"What do I wear to this basketball game date?" I ask, jumping right into why I called. No point in pleasantries, this is important.

"Emma, I thought something was wrong. You never call this early."

"That's because I'm never awake this early. What do I wear to a basketball date?"

"Isn't that tonight? You don't have to decide right now." Bella sounds sleepy and out-of-it.

"Hello, we are going to be at school all day. I have to be in the right outfit. It's not like we're coming home between school and the game. So, I repeat, what do I wear?" This time my voice goes up a little in desperation.

"Um, okay let me think." Bella knows my closet about as well, if not better, than I do. We bought most of it together on shopping excursions. "Jeans and your purple top, the one that is v-neck and a little tight."

"Which jeans?" I find the shirt she is referencing and hold it up, looking in the mirror. She's a genius, my friend the blonde.

"The really dark ones. Wear a necklace too."

"I don't know if I have a necklace that I like enough. I didn't even think about jewelry."

"Don't worry, I have that one you like with the purple teardrop stone in the middle. It'll be perfect. I'll bring that and you can wear it."

"You are the best."

"Okay, good." Bella yawns. "So can I go back to bed for another thirty minutes?"

"Don't ask me, I'm usually late. I don't know how this all works."

Bella laughs. "Alright, I'll see you at school. Bye."

One hot shower, Bella's perfectly picked outfit, and a quick bowl of oatmeal later I'm walking to school. I've decided to toss my phone into my backpack to keep a layer of protection between the technology and the chip, for safety. Now it's ringing and I cannot reach it. Me and my brilliant ideas.

I flip the backpack around so I'm wearing it on my chest and dig around in that tiny pocket on the front. Isn't it amazing how much stuff accumulates in that little space? Pencils, pens, sticks of gum, calculator, and finally my phone. I whip it out just as it stops ringing. Ugh, seriously?

The red banner tells me I missed 1 call from Tyler Garfield. Why in the world is Tyler calling me? I should probably call him back.

Before I can even finish the thought my phone is dialing. This malfunction thing in really removes all room for--

"Hey Emma, thanks for calling me back," Tyler answers.

"Hey, what did you need?"

"I don't really need it. I was just wondering if I can tag along with you and Bells to the basketball game tonight."

Tyler, my ex, wants to go with us to the basketball game date. Tyler, whose picture popped up randomly during my first strange date. How do I put this delicately? "Tyler, it's supposed to be like a date, isn't that kind of weird?"

"Em, how the heck is it a date? Alex is going to be playing basketball. Look, I like going, I just hate going alone."

"Well won't it be weird if he sees that we are together? I mean..." I can feel myself blushing "...we have a history. Plus that weird picture thing on the first date. He might get the wrong idea."

"I don't have to go. I guess. There's nothing else going on tonight, though. Bella will be with you, and Alex will be at the game, too. You guys are like my only friends."

Ow, he pulled out the guilt. He knows I hate the guilt. "Low blow, Ty. You have other friends."

"Not ones who love me enough to let me go to the game with them."

I feel myself caving in and let out an exasperated sigh. "You are impossible. You can tag along, but you have to make sure Alex knows it's just a friend thing."

"You're the best, Em. Thanks. Bye." Tyler hangs up.

I drop my phone back into the bag which I am still wearing the wrong way. As I flip it back around my mind starts processing. Let's recap. My first date with adorable eyes Alex was supposed to be a coffee shop date. Instead, he volunteered to attend a field hockey game with me, which is awesome of him. Alex was treated to a strange picture of Tyler, which made him somehow decide to befriend Tyler. In fact, Alex even decided to ask me on a second coffee date. The second date was cut short by basketball, but not before I earned an invitation to the next date.

So what if it's weird that this is going to be at a basketball game. Although I suppose It is weird that he's playing, I won't really even be with him. But basketball is obviously important to him and he wants me there.

No, I decide. Tyler is just jealous. This is definitely a date.

Chapter 17

"**HE SAW US,** right?" I'm standing on the bleachers between Bella and Tyler, jumping around like an idiot and cheering for the team. Alex just scored, again. Apparently he's pretty good because it's the second period and he's already scored eight times. That's good, I think.

"Em, he saw us. He has probably seen us a few times. He waved earlier." Tyler's voice makes me think he's probably rolling his eyes.

"He waved earlier. He saw us," Bella assures me.

Bella and I sit. When Tyler doesn't, I turn to look at him. "I thought you said we could get some food," he says. "I'm starving, let's go."

"Wait for intermission," I answer.

"Half time and no, the line would be huge. I'm going now. If you girls expect me to treat, you better come with." He's already headed down the stairs.

"How do we go now without making it seem like we followed for the free food?" Bella asks, a little giggle in her voice.

I get up and start following. "No idea but we have to hurry."

Bella and I chase after Tyler, laughing our heads off. We catch up to him at the concession stand line. I grab his elbow, panting to catch my breath from the laughs. He makes a big show of rolling his eyes at us, but he's smiling.

"Whew, we caught you. Good thing. We didn't want you to have to eat alone," I say trying to control my laughter.

"You didn't want to miss out on free food," Tyler corrects.

I pretend I'm offended, making a shocked noise and putting my hand on my chest. That sets all three of us into a huge fit of laughter. We are still laughing when the lady behind the counter clears her throat. The laughter trails off as we all turn our attention to her and notice that we are, in fact, next in line.

"Sorry, my friends here are comedians. Can we get three pretzels with cheese and three waters, please."

"Doesn't even need to ask what we want," Bella says, "yet never gets it wrong."

"I didn't even know I wanted a pretzel, but it sounds so good." I chuckle again, feeling silly.

The lady hands the food to Tyler, who hands it off to us one at a time. "$9.00." Bella and I watch as Tyler reaches out his right hand and taps the cash register.

"Oh my god, you got an account?" Bella shrieks.

Having paid already, Tyler turns and we all start walking back toward the bleachers. "Yeah, I went to the bank with my Dad a few days ago. All set."

"Wow, that's insane," Bella says.

Having a bank account nowadays is intense. With the use of phones, pay apps, and electronic banking all being tied to your chip you can basically do everything just by thinking about it. "So you memorized your account number or something and called that up when you paid just now?" I ask. Now that we're drawing close to legal banking age I'm especially curious about the details.

"Not exactly. The chip has all that. I just have to think about my Personal Identification Number. It's like pulling up the app on my phone to pay." Tyler shrugs. "It's pretty normal."

"You're just trying to act cool because you got it before us." Bella slaps Tyler on the arm. "We'll get it soon enough. Won't we Em?"

I can actually see the second she remembers. The face of total happiness and pure excitement, like a kid on Christmas, completely melts. Instead, she's the kid who thought it was green apple gelatin and just discovered the big spoonful is lime. "Oh my gosh, thank goodness you don't have one now with that stupid malfunction." You can tell she's trying to make it sound like a good thing.

"Malfunction?" Tyler stops short in the hallway and spins around.

I wasn't expecting it, so I crash right into him. "Good thing you got water bottles so I didn't spill on you, Ty. Geeze."

"What malfunction is she talking about?"

"My chip. The tests with Carl I told you about? Remember?"

"I remember he was running tests, yeah. Did you get the results?"

"Yes. He says it's malfunctioning." Seeing that Tyler doesn't plan to start walking again, I maneuver around him. "I don't want to talk about it."

We get back to our seats and I dig into my pretzel. They're being weird and quiet now, and it's annoying. I didn't want to think about this at all. Now we are all thinking about it. How I'll probably never be able to get a bank account because I'll accidentally pay for other people's crap. How I will always have to worry about projector plates.

"They're going to fix it though, Emma." Bella leans forward to see Tyler around me. "She's going to go to a neurologist."

"Oh, that's a good idea. Did you know they had a neurologist on the original team?" Tyler offers, "They'll know what to do."

"I don't want to talk about this," I remind them.

Tyler takes out his cell phone. Without asking, which is so completely like Tyler, he taps it to my right wrist.

It's my Dad, his manicured goatee and steel eyes. "Maybe. We can hope."

It plays on a loop.

After the third time, I yank my wrist away. "Satisfied?" I ask.

"Holy crap, Em. It just pulls up whatever you're thinking about?" Tyler asks.

"Not exactly. Sometimes it doesn't do it. I don't know. That's what malfunctioning means."

"Okay, sorry." He shoves pretzel into his mouth.

"It'll be great, Emma. You'll see. The neurologist will fix all of this and then everything will be fine again. We'll all be laughing about this in a few months," Bella says, "You'll see."

Yeah, yeah. They'll fix it.

All I know is, if I touched a projector plate right now it'd still be showing that same loop.

Chapter 18

I'M EARLY TO school. This has literally never happened. Did you know that if you get to school early enough they actually still have the doors locked? I have to sit on the front steps and wait until I see Mrs. Straightier walking in. When I finally see her, she is walking a little slow, probably because she has three large reusable grocery bags looped over her arms. "Good morning, Miss Johnson," she calls, surprise lighting up her face.

"Good morning. Let me take one of those." I reach my arms out. She deposits one bag. "I can probably take two."

"I suppose I do need to be able to unlock the door." She hands me a second bag. "Thank you, Emma."

In the classroom I slip into the back row, as usual. "You don't want to sit up front, Miss Johnson?" she asks.

Hell no. "No, thanks. I like the view of the screen from this angle."

The class eventually fills in the room. I'm playing with my Rubik's app. I decided that possibly having a malfunction was better than sitting here alone and bored. I lose track of time so I'm shocked when Mrs. Straightier clears her throat to start the class. I put my phone down and look around.

I don't see Alex. Weird. Maybe he's absent today.

Mrs. Straightier reminds everyone that we will be doing group presentations today. She taps the projector plate with her hand and the list of groups fills the screen. I'm third. Does my early arrival make sense now? I'm supposed to stand up in front of the entire class and project my presentation. With a fucking chip malfunction. Fantastic.

I lean into the aisle and find Bella. Great minds must think alike because she's turned around looking for me. I catch her eye and she gives me a thumbs-up.

I sit back and take a deep breath. My phone vibrates. "You'll be fine. We got this." It's Bella.

Reply. "I know. Thanks."

I continue to play with my phone, pushing the limits of my malfunction while the other groups present. I've prepared my slides, they're good. The question isn't, "will I earn an A", the question is more, "will my chip cooperate."

"Emma and Bella," Mrs. Straightier calls.

I get up, slipping my phone into my back pocket effortlessly, and start walking toward Bella. She meets me in the aisle. "Want to just send me the presentation and I can project it?" she asks.

It's a good idea. Technically we are each supposed to project at least six slides. Chances are we would lose a few points if Bella projected them all, but we'd do alright. Then again, I'm stubborn and I don't want this stupid malfunction running my life. "No, I will do my slides like I'm supposed to and you can take over."

"Okay." Bella hits me with that perfect smile. The one you can't help but smile back to.

I slowly walk to the projection plate. I take a deep breath and really focus on what I want to happen. Just my History presentation. Bring up my first slide. Please.

The Growth of the Euro, Negative Effects by Emma Johnson and Positive Effects by Annabella Norte.

The purple hue of the slide casts the front of the classroom in a glow like a neon grape. I let out the breath I was holding and speak loudly and clearly for the class as I mentally advance to my first slide.

It's going well. I manage to make it through slides one, two, and three. Everyone is listening. They laughed when it was appropriate. My eyes slip through the audience, they land on Alex. Alex who is row jumping. Alex who is randomly seated in the fourth row.

The projection skips. It blinks like a camera flashing, but in reverse. The light shuts off and then turns back on. It's enough to bring my full attention back to it. If I'm not careful here, I'll lose my presentation.

I refocus myself. Slide four, five, six. My last slide has some information the class has to record. I stand off to the side, smiling and waiting. I did it. I managed to make it through the presentation without a major malfunction. Soon I'll be able to give it the command to turn off. Right now it just has to stay frozen on the screen.

I risk another glance at Alex. He looks in my direction and turns up the smile that melts my heart. I squirm to avoid bouncing on my toes and smile back. He drops his eyes back to his paper, recording my notes.

95

He's not mad. Maybe he sat closer because he knew we were presenting today. He wanted to be able to see the presentations. Class presentation days are always strange. They don't have to follow the rules of the regular days. Maybe row jumping is allowed. Maybe he'll ask me to go out on another date with him. Maybe we'll share a milkshake or something old school like that.

Maybe he'll wrap me up in his arms after we share the ice cream treat and pull me close. Tell me that I have ice cream on my lip. Use it as an excuse to kiss me passionately, right there in the ice cream shop no matter who's looking. Alex will be the kind of kisser who curls your toes.

The laughter is what I notice first. Then I notice the purple hue is gone. I already know before I turn my head, but I can't avoid looking. I have to know how bad it is. Sure enough, the screen is now frozen on the image of Alex and I locked in a passionate kiss. It's a fantasy image, bearing the watery edges of the background. Nothing else is clear, but there is no doubt who it is up there on the screen or what they are doing.

I can't figure out how to react. I'd like to run from the room, but this is my presentation. Instead, I beg my chip to turn the screen off. Just a black screen, just a black screen. Finally, it complies. I walk to the other side of the classroom, still in the front but as far away from the plate as I can get.

Bella, ever the professional, steps up and clears her pretty little throat. "Sorry for that interruption, I'm not sure what happened there. I'm sure you'll all be understanding about it. Now let's get back on track." She taps the projection plate and her pink glow fills the front of the room. I manage to make it through all of Bella's slides without crying, dying, or looking for Alex. I know my face is red, I can feel the burning. I know I'm sweating. I want to run away and hide under a rock. I want to disappear. I kind of wish someone would invent a chip that would let you do that, disappear on command. Of course mine would probably malfunction and then I'd just be wandering the halls thinking I was invisible.

The second I hear Bella's final slide I jog to Mrs. Straightier. "Can I use the restroom?" I ask.

She hands me the pass, which she already had in her hand, with an almost apologetic smile. "Take as long as you need, sweetheart," she whispers.

On the way out of the classroom, I grab my backpack. I'll need that, since I'm not planning on coming back. I text Bella from the hallway. "Going home, this day sucks. Thanks for finishing."

"We'll probably get our A anyway," she replies.

Reply. "Suddenly doesn't seem as important."

"It must be, you stayed."

Reply. "Just supporting a friend."

I hear the ding of a cell phone echo through the hallway. I turn around to see who else is in the hallway and the tears just start flowing like someone turned on a faucet. It's Bella. Perfect attendance, straight A Bella. She's in the hallway instead of class. For me. "What are you doing out here?"

"Just supporting a friend." She wraps her arms around my shoulders and steers me toward the bathroom. "We'll figure this out."

Chapter 19

"**BELLS, YOU CAN** say what you want, but you can't argue with the facts. That was obviously us in that fantasy projection. He is never going to speak to me again," I say. I'm flopped on my back on the floor of my bedroom. This is where Bella and I fled to after she talked me into surviving a day of sniggers and sideways glances. There's an empty pint of chocolate chip cookie dough ice cream next to me, dripping the remnants of the delicious white sugary mix onto my carpet.

"Okay it was obviously you, I'll give you that. But Alex never speaking to you again is not a fact. You don't know that. He could've been flattered, Em." Bella is sitting on my bed, legs wrapped delicately underneath her. She looks like she could close her eyes and slip into meditation at any second.

I sigh. Alex is only part of the problem. If my chip keeps malfunctioning like this, there will be a string of these bad experiences everywhere I go. "What if they can't fix it?"

Bella gets up off the bed and lays down next to me. "They have to."

We lay that way for awhile. The sun starts to set and brings a weird darkness to the room, forcing me to get up and flip the light on. "Okay, we sat and sulked long enough," I say. "What's our next move?"

Bella sits up. "Let's call Tyler."

"Why?"

"I don't know, why not? He seems like a good person to call. He loves this tech stuff." Bella is already reaching for my projector remote. The screen in my wall wakes up, turning white with her touch. She must command it to call Tyler because the text, "dialing Tyler Garfield," scrolls across the screen.

There's a whooshing sound when the call connects and Tyler's brooding brown eyes fill the screen. "Oh, you're both there. Hi ladies."

"Hey Ty," Bella greets. "Did you hear about what happened in History today?"

"Wow, you're just gonna jump right into it, aren't you, Bells?" I cringe.

"Yeah," he answers, "I heard you two rocked your presentation." He hits me with a smile. It only kind of makes me feel better.

"How bad is it?" I ask. "He's never gonna talk to me again, right?"

"I don't know, Em. Maybe he'll be flattered," Tyler says.

"Oh my gosh, that is exactly what I said." Bella smacks me on the shoulder. "Isn't that what I said?"

"That is what she said," I concede. "Ty, how serious is this malfunction though? Like, now that you've seen what it does and stuff."

"Without studying it or anything I can say it's unusual. But I'm not really concerned. If it were me, I'd want them to try resetting it. Even if the neurologist can't remove it, maybe you have options. I'm saying don't give up, Emma."

"Okay, thanks Tyler." I have to admit I'm starting to feel a little better. Bella can say all she wants about how this is going to work out, but she's just farting rainbows. Tyler knows about this stuff so his positivity holds more weight.

"Let's talk about something else," Bella says. "Remember the year all three of us went on the ski trip?" Every single year Bella's family goes skiing in Colorado over the Christmas break from school. I regularly tag along, but only once has Tyler's Mom let him come too. That was almost two years ago.

"Is that trip on again this year?" Tyler asks.

"Absolutely. Are you guys coming?"

"I am sure my parents will let me," I answer.

"I'll start working on Mom now," Tyler answers. "We deserve that much fun again. Do you remember when Bella ripped her jeans on the slope?"

"Oh my gosh, you make it sound like I was trying to ski in jeans. I was not." Bella blushes.

"It doesn't matter. You were walking around on the slope and you ripped your jeans." I laugh.

"I was walking past the slope and I slipped and they ripped." Bella is laughing now too.

"Worth watching again," Tyler says. On screen a smaller window opens up in the bottom right corner. Tyler must be sharing a projection with us.

The POV must be Tyler's. The ground is covered in a thick blanket of snow and skiers are everywhere. Bella and I are walking in front of

Tyler. We are both wearing thick ski jackets over our jeans. I am wearing snow boots, Bella is wearing Converse.

We walk along for a bit. I start to feel guilty that Tyler is behind us, instead of next to us. How often does he do this? Then the POV seems to focus more on my butt. It almost zooms in a little. It's embarrassing, but I notice my butt looks pretty good. In fact, I look pretty good in this memory. My hair is shiny and long. My jeans fit perfectly. I should probably dig through my closet and find those jeans.

Bella slips. I knew it was going to happen, since I lived this memory, but it still makes my arms shoot out toward her like I'm going to catch her. On screen me slips as well, because we had our arms linked. But Bella is the only one to fall on her butt. Tyler reaches us, holding his own ski jacketed arms down to her. "Are you alright?" he asks, his voice echoing because it's in his head and said out loud.

"Yeah." Bella lets herself be pulled up and then reaches her hands around behind her. "Oh my gosh, you guys. I think they're ripped." She turns around. I actually laugh again. I can't help it. Bella's perfect dark skinny jeans are ripped right along the pocket, revealing her unicorn covered underwear.

This time real Bella laughs too. "At least you guys didn't make me walk to the lodge with my butt showing," she says. "Thanks for crowding in and covering me."

"Hey, that's what friends do. We cover for each other in embarrassing situations," Tyler says. He's not looking at Bella though, he's looking at me. I'm thinking about how we just saw a video of him checking out my butt, so I'm blushing. I wonder if he's thinking about it too.

"Alright ladies, I'd love to sit here and chat with you but I have stuff to do. I'll talk to you both tomorrow." Tyler flashes us a peace sign and the screen goes dark.

"Feeling any better?" Bella asks.

"Actually, yeah. You two are good for my brain," I answer.

"Good. I have to get going too, love. I'll talk to you later. Call me." Bella is out my door before I can protest. I'm left alone in my darkening bedroom to wonder what I would do without friends. With any luck, I'll never have to find out.

Then again, I don't really know how long someone with a chip malfunction can manage to keep close friends in this society. I'm literally an outcast, dragging them down with me.

Chapter 20

I **HONESTLY CAN'T** remember the last time I've taken a sick day from school. Does it count that I'm not actually sick today? I'm pacing around the house waiting until the time comes for my appointment with the neurologist. This morning when I woke up, late, I thought it seemed like a good idea to stay home until the time came. Now I'm regretting it. At least in class I'd have assignments, other people, and possible embarrassment to keep my mind occupied.

"Emma, stop running around the living room. I'm trying to get some work done," Dad scolds. He has been seated in front of the projector adding numbers to some document for hours. It's making me crazy.

"I'm not running. I'm walking."

"You're doing a lot of walking. Be productive if you have to walk. Go outside or something."

"Dad, I'm supposed to be home sick. I can't be seen parading around the neighborhood during school hours."

"You have a doctor's appointment, the absence is legitimate."

"Doesn't feel that way," I mumble.

"Emma," Dad uses his stern parent voice, "I am trying to work here." He gestures to the garbled characters on the screen. "I would appreciate some time to concentrate."

"Fine." I flop into the reclining chair as far away from the projector as I possibly can get. Maybe I can learn something about brilliance by watching him work. Open on the screen is a document that presumably shows the results of some kind of trial. There are patient initials, a column labeled results, and lots and lots of numbers. I have no idea what this could be a trial for or what kind of results we are looking at.

Dad is adding what I suppose are factual sentences to a column labeled analysis. He continues to stare at the screen with rapt attention, much like I would watch an internet video of the latest Local Evolution song. But I can tell he is processing the data because the column occasionally fills with a sentence like "the patient does not exhibit a change that is statistically significant" or "patient may have outside factors, refer to other medications list".

When Dad mentally types like this I notice he forgoes all grammatical rules. There are no capital letters and very little punctuation. I happen to know that you can mentally type and follow all rules, so this must be a deliberate choice he is making. Odd.

"Hey Dad, why are you using all lowercase letters?" I ask.

The sentence he is working on never even slows down. I certainly can't bother him enough to get the screen to turn black. He is not listening.

104

"What, Emma?" he asks, once the sentence is finished. The screen stays bright.

"Nothing. Never mind." It really doesn't matter anyway, I was only making conversation.

We continue in this way for as long as I can possibly stand it... so about ten minutes. Then I decide it's time to get my head examined. "Dad, it's time for the appointment."

That earns his attention. The projector screen goes black as Dad turns around to face me. "Is it really that late already?"

"Yup. Can we just get this over with, please?"

Dad shuts off the screen and grabs his keys. "Let's do this."

'This' turns out to be nothing like I expected. There's a lot of hurry-up-and-wait going on, which is my least favorite activity. When you're already nervous waiting is the worst thing to ask you to do. Dad and I have to do a lot of it. We wait in the waiting room, even though we were on time for my appointment. We wait a little more after the apology explaining that the neurologist is dealing with a patient emergency and is therefore running a little behind.

Then she calls my name and we move to the smaller room. To wait. Unbelievable. I'm seriously considering running away in my sad little cotton gown that barely reaches my knees. I'm freezing too. Who makes you wear paper and then turns the temperature down and leaves you? Where are these people?

There's a tiny knock at the door. Thank God. "Come in," I say. My anger dissipates and the nerves kick back in. My knees instantly start jostling. I force myself to stop that, it makes the paper underneath me crinkle like a potato chip bag.

"Hi Emma, I'm Amanda. I'm going to take you for a scan of your arm and your brain today. Is that alright with you?" the lady asks. She is young, brunette, perky. She's wearing bright pink scrubs and a gigantic smile.

"Sure." Would anyone ever actually tell this nurse that it's not okay? I made the appointment but no, you're not allowed to do anything. Give me a break.

I follow her down the hallway labeled with test names I've heard on doctor shows; CAT scan, MRI, X-ray. My feet are bare and it makes a weird slapping noise. Also the floor is very cold. I make a mental note to bring slippers along next time. Dear lord, I'm thinking about there being a next time. I roll my eyes. Let's try to get this all done in one shot.

We reach a room marked x-ray. She leads me in and tells me to sit on a stool. I watch as she sets up the giant camera with the slate panels that will hold the images. "Are you wearing any metal?" she asks.

Where would I have hidden metal? In my underwear? "Nope, just the chip."

"Those are plastic, mostly. Completely safe." Smile. She has me stand in front of the big board with my arm up. "Try to stand very still." She smiles again. Do you think it's instinct to smile that much or is she forcing it?

She goes into a little room connected by a pane of glass to the room I'm in. If the radiation is not safe for her to even be in the same room, what does that say about where I'm standing? I have to seriously restrain myself from bouncing on my toes.

"Alright Emma, take a deep breath and hold it please," she says.

I'm guessing I was moving. I do as she instructs.

There's a popping sound from the machine. Nurse pink is back, pulling the cartridges out and, in what is becoming slightly annoying, smiling. "Alright, ready for the next one?"

I shrug, because I'm not sure what else she expects me to do. I follow her down the cold hallway again. This time I try to make my feet slap as loud as they can. She doesn't turn around.

We walk into the room labeled MRI. The first thing I notice is the giant white donut looking machine with a long board sticking out. The nurse asks me to lay down. I sit on the edge and give her a strange look. I've never done this before. "You'll have to put your head near the entrance, honey," she tells me as she lays her hand on my upper arm and lightly pushes like she is reclining me.

"The entrance to the room?" I ask.

"To the machine." She points to the white donut. By following her arm I notice that they are, in fact, connected. How did I not see that before? So maybe not a donut. Maybe a round monster sticking out his tongue.

I lay down in such a way that my hair would be brushing up against his teeth, if he had teeth. Oh man, I hope he doesn't have teeth. "Emma, just relax. This is not as bad as anyone thinks it will be. You're going to lay very still. The machine is going to do its work and then it'll be all over. Just close your eyes, relax, and let me get clear pictures. Okay?" She whisks away so that I can't see her anymore.

Then the machine begins to move. I squeeze my eyes shut and concentrate on breathing. It's not so bad, at first. Calming actually. I like quiet spaces and I like sleep. Except I can't sleep in here. Plus I'm not supposed to move to get comfortable.

I feel an itch start in my leg. I squeeze my eyes a little tighter. This isn't real, my brain only thinks my leg is itchy. It's not. Don't think about it. Don't think about that itchy spot. You got this. How much longer? I just want to scratch my leg.

The tube starts to feel smaller. I want to open my eyes to make sure that the walls aren't closing in around me. I think I even try to open them. My fear is getting the upper hand, they won't open. Is it getting hotter in here? I think it's getting hot. How much longer? What is she doing?

I swallow and it sounds more like a gulp. Gosh my leg is really itchy now. What if there's like a bug crawling around on my leg and it's biting me? Okay, now I really need to open my eyes.

That was a bad idea. With my eyes open I can see how close the tube is. It's big and oppressive and very close to me. My breathing picks up speed. I think this may be what a panic attack is. My heart is racing. I actually have to lick my lips to occupy my mouth so I can't scream. I take a big breath in.

The machine starts moving again. Everything calms as I emerge back into the room. The air feels so much cooler, like it's moving freely out here. "See, that wasn't so bad, was it?" the nurse asks.

It was awful, terrible, agonizing. I never, ever want to do that again. "I guess not," I answer. It's not really her fault and I don't need to be a wimp, right?

Back to the little room. "I'm going to go bring in your father. You can get dressed. The neurologist will be along to tell you what she sees on our tests soon."

"You get the tests back that fast?" The question kind of blurts out of my mouth.

"We are a state of the art facility, honey. We process right here," she answers. Then she shuts the door.

I dress fast. How embarrassing would it be to have the nurse and Dad come into the room when I'm standing around in my bra or something? Turns out I didn't have to dress that quickly. More sitting and waiting.

When Dad joins me the nurse promises it will only be a minute.

That is a lie, but one I'm expecting. We sit and we wait. Dad pulls out his phone after a few minutes and starts playing around with it. I never ask what he's doing and I don't pull out my own.

Finally there's a knock on the door. The woman who blows into the room like a tornado is nothing like her cotton candy sweet nurse. For one there is nothing lovable or squeezable about this lady. She's all angles and elbows. Her hair is trying to escape from her stern bun. Her mouth looks like it has never smiled a day in her life.

"I'm Doctor Angelo and I've reviewed your tests," she greets. She makes no attempt to shake hands or learn our names. She never even sits, just kind of leans on the counter with her hip. "Your chip has become embedded in your neurological system. I'm afraid of doing damage to your brain function by trying to removing it. I see nothing wrong with your brain functions, so that is good news. It means whatever is wrong is truly with your chip and not with your brain. However, I would not feel comfortable getting the chip out of your wrist."

"Are there other options?" I ask.

"Not from me." She looks from me to Dad and her eyes linger there a second. She looks uncomfortable. Then, without another word, she backs out of the room.

It's all over before I can even fully process what it means. That's it? She's just giving up? She can't help? "Dad, what are we supposed to do now?" I ask. My eyes are filling with tears and my vision is cloudy.

Dad rubs the hairs on his chin, thinking. "Carl thought he noticed a trigger file abnormality. We can let him reload that. Basically it's a computer malfunction, we can work on a few things." Dad stands up. "Don't lose hope yet." He tries for a smile.

Besides the obvious, I see a new problem. I'm perfectly aware that sometimes, when you can't fix it, computer malfunctions equal throw out the machine and buy a new computer.

Chapter 21

IT'S A NEW day. Bella says I have to establish a new normal, so that's my goal. I'm awake early, even though it's a Saturday. I get dressed and I eat breakfast. I sit on the couch and read a book, like a real one, not an e-book. I wait for Dad to holler at me that it's time to head into Phoenix again. It's nice to have time to read, I actually get lost in the book for awhile. I may have a chip malfunction that can't be removed, but at least I can just avoid technology. No one is making me wear a big red emblem of my curse on all my clothing.

Once we are in the car Dad and I resume the painfully silent routine. I've left my phone at home, new normal and all, so I have nothing to do and no one to talk to. Boring. Maybe part of my new normal should be carrying the book around so I always have something to do.

We park and enter the lobby. The security guard makes us sign in. This time Carl is walking into the building right behind us. He badges past security and all three of us pile into the elevator. Dad and Carl stand right before the doors. I'm happy to hide behind them.

"Steve, are you still okay with all of this?" Carl asks.

"I am."

"The upload we discussed, that is still fine with you?"

"We need to work from a full set of data. We can't trust that she is giving us everything."

Carl nods. My eyes get a little wider. What are the odds that they are talking about someone else? Is there a risk to whatever trigger file Carl has to reload?

The elevator doors open. Dad heads directly for the chairs in the lobby. Carl turns and smiles at me. Oh look, he does remember that I'm here. "Alright Emma, follow me." He heads off down the same hallway we walked last time. I follow him, nerves and all.

I plop myself down into the same chair I sat in the last time I was here, before I'd heard the word malfunction. I wait for Carl to produce the cards from the pocket of his sports blazer, but he doesn't. Instead, he immediately sits down and begins typing away on the old machine. I'd like to watch what he's typing, but the screen is in the same position as last time, angled away from me. With nothing else to look at in this room, I watch Carl.

Last time I was here I noticed his eyes were dark, this time I can tell they're actually blue. Maybe they're that kind that change color with your outfit. He is wearing a blue button down shirt, open a little at the collar and a sport coat in place of the vest. Today he looks more professional, yet somehow younger and more handsome as well.

He is still typing away. I'm starting to think he forgot I'm here. I clear my throat.

"One more second, Emma. We just need to wait for this to load." He sits back and threads his hands together behind his head. "How's school been?" he asks.

"Fine." Despite this embarrassing malfunction crap that I have yet to figure out.

"That's good. I always liked school." The silence balloons up again. Carl wiggles the mouse on the machine like someone impatient would push a walk button at a crosswalk. Repeating the action in hopes it will encourage faster speeds.

"Alright, it's done," he finally announces. He spins the computer monitor toward me. "I'm going to play a quick video. You are going to try and interrupt. We will see if last time was a fluke."

So last time I was able to interrupt?

"Ready, Emma?"

I nod. I'm as ready as I'm going to get. A video starts on the screen. Something about nature. It actually looks pretty cool. I close my eyes. How can I interrupt if I'm thinking about the video he's watching? Instead I think about the book. I wonder if Hester wanted a single moment of happiness, like a fling. Did she mean to end up pregnant and attached to this guy? It sure seems like she loves him, but then again she is able to be away from him while she is being shunned. He is the one who seems the most upset by her punishment. I wonder if there is someone like that out there for everyone. Someone to worry about them more than they worry about themselves.

"Thanks, Emma," Carl says.

I open my eyes to see that my interruption was successful, although confusing. The screen is filled with a picture of Tyler. I'd love to wonder what the implications of that are about, but there is something more pressing drawing my attention. Along the bottom of the screen there are green things. Like numbers and letters all mixed together in this glaringly obvious glowing green. "What are those things? They've never been there before."

Carl looks where my finger is pointing. "Just location and date stamps. It's always there, it's usually invisible. I brought it forward for our purposes today." He shrugs.

I find it odd that he didn't bring the strange text forward last time, if it's important. But I guess maybe he's trying something new. Of course I was able to interrupt again, so the something new is not exactly working.

Carl's phone rings. He pulls it out of his jacket pocket and glances at the screen. "Excuse me, I should take this." He steps out as he puts it up to his ear.

I don't know why the picture of Tyler is still on the screen. Honestly, I don't even know why it came up. I wasn't thinking about Ty. I was thinking about a book. Pictures of those characters or the author would make sense. Tyler isn't exactly the local town reverend I picture when I read that book. I glance back toward the door to make sure Carl is not returning. I don't hear anything. I reach for the old fashioned mouse and move it around the screen. The picture fades away, like a screensaver would. Weird.

I sit back down and sigh. How long is this phone call gonna take? I look back at the screen. Along the bottom there are windows that must be reduced, hanging out there waiting to be viewed again. One says, "Inbox 118." Yikes Carl, check your email. Another one says, "Tests." It's green, like a spreadsheet. Is that the one Dad was using the other day? It had test results Dad was analyzing and adding conclusions for. Maybe they're doing some new study together.

Again I strain to hear what is happening in the hallway. I think

I'm almost hoping to hear something, just to give me something to do. I'm so bored. I tap out a random rhythm on my leg, not sure what it's the beat for. My eyes land on the "Tests" tab again. It can't hurt to open it and peek, Dad had it open right in front of me.

I reach for the mouse again, clicking to open the spreadsheet. This is not the same file. Guilt pours in. If this is not Dad's file then I should not be looking at it. I should close it.

There are only three columns on this one, headings read "name, file uploaded, and date." File uploaded? What the heck does that mean? I should really close it.

I scroll all the way down, past the hundred or so rows of names. People who have had some kind of file uploaded, even though Dad claims there have never been any other malfunctions. Is he wrong? Was he lying? Do these people have files uploaded for other reasons?

All the way at the bottom my eyes land on the final name. Immediately, my heart jumps to my throat.

Emma Johnson. File 14.3b. December 12.

What the crap is file 14.3b? I tap my wrist on the connection plate, thinking I need a search for the text 14.3b. A small box opens in the top right corner. "14.3b results 1 of 1." Suddenly I'm feeling sick.

Whatever this file is that they uploaded, I'm the only person who's ever needed it.

Chapter 22

UPLOADED FILES. DOESN'T that imply something was somehow put onto my chip? But I never touched the stupid old fashioned tower thing, at least not until I needed to search for text. Wait, that means I interrupted without touching it either. Did this 14.3b file thing give me a longer range? That's not helpful. That's the opposite of helpful, actually.

I hold my hand out toward my wall projector plate. It's pretty far from my position scrunched up in my bed, so I can't reach it. I think about the book. How I'd like to see facts about the author. Nothing happens.

Maybe I'm still too far away. I scramble out of bed, all hopes of getting any good sleep today completely squashed anyway. I walk to where I would normally stand for my projector, then I take two large steps backwards. I'm close to my bed, but now I'm at the right angle. I think about pulling up the history replay I should be studying.

Nothing happens.

I step closer. Try again.

Nothing.

I step closer, now standing where I know I should be able to project.

Mrs. Straightier is standing before the class and the slide behind her clearly reads "Eurasia." This is what I meant to recall, so that's good. There's only one minor problem. The bottom of the screen is aglow with green characters.

I back away, breaking the connection. What in the world is going on here? Good thing I live with a tech guy. I dash down the stairs, intent on finding Dad. His office door is open, meaning we're welcome to disturb him. I can hear Mom humming something from the kitchen. As soon as I step into the office, Dad's eyes leave what he's doing and land on my face.

"Good morning, Emma. How are you doing today?" he greets.

"Fine. Hey Dad, I have these weird green letters and stuff on the bottom of my projections." I tap his screen while thinking about the History lesson. The image appears, green characters and all. "What are those?"

"What did Carl say they were?" Dad wiggles a little in his seat. It lets out an odd squeak, like it needs oil.

"Um, he said they were always there but he brought them forward." I put my hand down, releasing my connection. His screen goes black.

"Oh." Dad wiggles again. He looks uncomfortable. "Then that's what they are, Emma. He just forgot to shut them off." He hits me with his Dad look, the one that makes me squirm. "He probably intended to before you ran off."

"I didn't run off." Okay, I kind of did. "Whatever, can you shut them off?" I throw my arm out in indication of his computer tower. It's not like you need a special machine to do this stuff. I don't know why Dad insists on me seeing Carl instead of just having him do everything right here.

"Emma, just leave it be. You'll get used to it." He drops his gaze down toward his desk and begins shuffling papers.

I know it's the signal that I'm being dismissed. But I can't leave. I want to ask him about the file upload. How do I broach the topic of the spreadsheet that I never should have seen? I sigh a little.

The noise brings Dad's eyes back to my face. "Can you shut the door when you leave, Emma?" he asks.

I can hear a knock on the front door. Hear Mom shouting, "I'll get it."

"Actually, there was something else I was gonna ask you, Dad." I still don't know how I'm going to get the details out without incriminating myself for snooping.

"Emma," Mom hollers from the hallway, "Tyler and Bella are here."

"Tell me later, Emma. You have guests." Dad returns his eyes to his papers. "Remember to shut the door on your way out."

I think about defying him. I think about blurting out some question like, "What is fourteen point three b?" and seeing what his reaction will be. Before I can work up the guts, Tyler and Bella are in the doorway behind me.

"Hi Em." Tyler smiles. "Ready to study?"

I make the decision to leave, shutting the stupid door behind me. In the hallway I plaster on my nothing-to-worry-about smile. "I'm ready. Let's go use my projector."

"Are you alright using technology?" Bella asks as we turn to head back up the stairs in a single-file line that would've made my kindergarten teacher swoon.

"It's just in front of you guys. You won't judge me if something goes wrong." Right?

We all file into my room. Bella drops onto the end of my bed, pulling her legs up underneath her. She pulls her perfectly flagged little spiral notebook out of a backpack and slides a purple ink pen from inside the spirals. Tyler stands stiff in the doorway, unsure of where he should sit. He could sit on the floor, which is likely uncomfortable, or he could sit on the bed. But it's my bed. It's the bed we made out on a few times. That's probably uber awkward. "I'll go grab some chairs," I offer. Tyler visibly relaxes.

In the kitchen Mom is making something that smells like cinnamon. I pause long enough to fill my nostrils. We will have to come back down for whatever that is later, I decide. The thing about friends and cinnamon is they both make me feel more at ease. So much so that when I reenter my bedroom lugging a heavy wooden kitchen chair I already feel a little better. Tyler drops into the chair and I head to the projector plate. "Alright, are we all set?" I ask. When they both nod, I tap the plate.

The History replay starts. Mrs. Straightier is standing before the "Eurasia" slide again. "Remember what we have learned about successful civilizations," she is saying. "You can judge them based on five things; religion, art, language, technology, and government. We will analyze..."

I realize I don't have anything to write with. I cross over to the other side of my room, knowing the video will play until it's end so long as I don't interrupt or tell it to stop. I grab a few pens and a notebook. I flop onto my stomach along the top of the bed, near my pillows. My head is behind Bella, but I can see.

Tyler turns around in his chair. "Em, why are you recording this?" he asks.

"What? I'm not recording it. I mean it's a memory so I guess it was sort of recorded at the time." What is he talking about?

"Can you two please shush? I'm checking to make sure I have all these notes," Bella growls.

Tyler tries to hide his laugh at Bella's expense by clearing his throat. I'm sure she doesn't buy it. I don't. He sort of stands up and angles his chair so he can see us and the screen. He points his right arm out toward the bottom of the screen. "Those are log file size counters and they're incrementing."

"Tyler, is that English?" I ask.

Tyler stands up and walks to the wall. "This piece right here is recording the size of the file." He points to the far right, toward a set of numbers that are ticking up as the video continues to play. "I'm guessing this other piece is the date it was made, since this next piece is today's date." His finger moves along the bottom as he explains. "Here's the time. This might be our GPS coordinates right now, or maybe of where you were when it recorded. I'm not entirely sure." He locks eyes with me. "But for sure someone is recording this and I wondered why."

"Carl told me that information is always running in the background. He said he brought it forward so he could see it during our session today." Somehow it sounds empty now, like a lie.

"Okay, I guess." Tyler backs off and squints at the screen. He shoves his hands deep into the pockets of his jeans. "Em, that doesn't make sense." He gets that look, like he's frustrated. "Your chip wouldn't have any need to recall or record GPS coordinates."

"You just said you only think they're GPS coordinates." Still, my stomach is starting to squirm.

Tyler throws his hands up in defeat. "Alright, that's true. I just thought it was strange. It doesn't all add up for me is all I'm saying." Join the club, it sure doesn't add up for me either. I get the feeling we're not playing with all the data here.

"Do we have all that figured out now?" Bella asks, her voice dripping with annoyance. "Can we please rewind? I missed the last like ten minutes of notes."

I stand and cross my room to comply with her request. Tyler drops back into the chair. He looks skeptical, like giving in on this argument was not what he truly wanted to do. Armed with my new lingo from Tyler, I need to find an excuse to go talk to Dad again. "I smell cinnamon. I'm gonna go see what Mom is cooking down there."

"I hope it's those awesome sticky buns." Bella licks her lips.

Tyler doesn't react, he's still staring at the numbers on the screen like he's analyzing. Maybe he'll figure it out. Meanwhile, I'm gonna go ask the guy who probably already knows.

Five minutes later, armed with a plate of four of Mom's famous sticky buns, I'm standing outside the closed door to Dad's office again. I know I have to have the courage to just throw the door open and enter. I can't stand here too long before I do it, either. I imagine the smell of cinnamon forming tendrils that curl up under the door and inch closer to Dad's nostrils. Soon he'll know the cinnamon is coming from outside the room.

Without knocking, which could give him the opportunity to deny me entrance, I fling the door open. Dad's face registers the shock, then his hand moves to tap the screen. But I saw it. At least, I think I did. I'm thrown off for a minute.

My gaze falls on the plate of rolls. "Oh sorry, Mom said to bring you a roll. I probably should've knocked." I try to look sheepish.

Dad grins. "Oh, I'll take one. I love those things."

I drop a napkin from my right hand onto his desk and hold out the plate so he can choose a roll. "Hey Dad, I also wanted to ask you one more time to please turn off these green things."

"Emma, we talked about this--"

"I know. But even Tyler says it weird. You like Tyler, remember? He's a good guy. He says they're like recording. It makes me nervous. What if there are other techy people out there who know what it means and I like play a video during class or something? I just want it turned off. Please." It's as much begging as I can muster around the lump that has formed in my throat.

"Emma Jean," the Dad voice is fully active now. He is not happy with me. "They are tiny characters on the bottom of a projection. You will be ignoring them in no time at all. Now I have data to analyze from an ongoing study. Shut the door behind you."

I can't argue. Not after what I saw when I came in. I turn and leave the room, shutting the door behind me. I don't know what to think anymore. I can't exactly ask Dad about file 14.3b and expect an honest answer. I wouldn't be giving him new information. He was just looking at Carl's spreadsheet, I'm sure of it.

Chapter 23

—▪——▪———▪———▪———▪———▪———▪———▪———▪———▪———▪———▪——

IN AN EFFORT to acclimate myself to my new normal, I did not use the alarm on my phone this morning. Okay, so I probably didn't use the alarm on my phone because I hate alarms. Either way, I overslept again. This is a problem because that History test we were studying for is happening first period, at 8 AM.

So that explains how I wound up jogging to school again.

I managed to squeeze myself into the door to History 7 minutes late. Nowhere near my latest arrival ever. Mrs. Straightier looked right at me as I slipped in. The chair on the row was taken so I had to squeeze by some guy and drop myself into the second one over. It was awkward. I'm sure the whole class noticed. The weird thing is Mrs. Straightier kept on going like I never interrupted.

She even walked back after the test was handed out. I thought the verbal lashing was coming. Instead, she smiled at me and walked away. File this under weirdest morning ever.

The History test turns out to be pretty standard. In my opinion, it's too easy. The guy who plopped his butt into my seat must not think so, judging by how much he used his phone under the desk. Lame.

Finished with time to spare I let my eyes wander around the room. From this seat I can actually see Bella, she appears to be done as well. I look up and down my row, Alex's row. He is nowhere to be found. I haven't actually seen him since the whole kissing video incident. Oh great, Em, get thinking about that topic. Now my stomach hurts.

My cell phone is turned off, wrapped in a sock, but hiding at the bottom of my backpack. I decided if some emergency happened even a girl living a new normal would need a phone. I fish it out, flip it to vibrate, and turn it on. I open a text message to Bella. "Do you see Alex anywhere?"

I can actually see her try and be sly about digging her phone out of her backpack when she feels it vibrate against her calf. I almost laugh at her. She turns her little blonde head around, clearly searching for him. "Fourth row, opposite side from me."

Oh yeah, there he is. Reply. "Is he still testing?"

Her head turns again. "Nope, doesn't look like it. He's on his phone."

I decide to seize the moment. I could sit here and wonder if he's completely offended or if he's flattered, as Tyler suggested, or I can just ask the source. I open a text. "Hey Alex, it's Emma. How's it going?"

From here, sitting behind him, I can't actually see a difference. I mean, it's the back of his head. I wait. Finally, the phone buzzes. "Good. You?"

Reply. "I'm alright. Look I wanted to apologize for that thing last week. It was honestly out of my control. I can explain more if you want.

Maybe get coffee again?"

This time the wait is even longer, likely owing to my longer text. My stomach really hurts. I'm compensating by bouncing my knees. The guy next to me must be annoyed, he keeps dramatically sighing. Whatever, dude, you cheated on the test. My phone vibrates. "Don't worry about it, I'm alright."

What the heck does that mean? Reply. "So is that a no on the coffee?" I follow it up with a cute emoticon, just because.

The vibration comes fast. "I think we should just be friends."

Oh. I put my phone back down on the desk. Friends. I have some of those. I have two of those, actually. I have a feeling Alex doesn't want to be another one. Alex wants to be done with me. Of course he does. I'm the girl who projected a fantasy of making out with him in front of the entire History class. I'm the girl who popped a picture of some other dude up on her phone during our date. I'm the girl whose chip is malfunctioning, even if he doesn't know that.

I hold the power button down, turning off my phone, and return it to its safe little nest. I spend what is left of my History class staring off into the expanse. Friends.

"Emma, what happened to your phone? I texted you again." Bella has managed to find me leaving History. Despite the fact that she moves slow and I was consciously moving fast, she even caught up. She loops her skinny little arm through mine and drops her voice to a whisper, "Did you have another incident with the phone?"

This is what friends are, Alex Slater. People who know everything about you and don't judge you for it. People who understand the malfunction and cut you some slack for it. "No, I just put it away," I answer. "Alex and I were done talking."

"Oh, okay." I'm sure she notices my tone is odd. "What did you talk about?" she pushes.

"He just wants to be friends." I let that hang between us. I can imagine it reverberating like we are in a deep, dark canyon somewhere.

"Oh. What the hell?" she asks.

I can't help it. I'm trying to be angry here but my perfect princess of a best friend just cursed in the hallway of our school, kind of loudly. It's so out of character that it makes me chuckle.

"I mean, it was just a stupid fantasy. I bet every single person in this school has them. Heck, if someone showed a fantasy video of kissing me I'd be flattered," she says.

"So if Marcus got up there in front of the whole History class and projected a video of making out with you, that would be okay with you?"

"Yeah!" Bella moves her hands a lot when she gets excited. She slips her arm out of mine as she warms up to that. "Oh my gosh, can you imagine? Here I am spending my time fantasizing about Marcus and then he steps up and shows the whole class he does the same thing? That would be amazing! Better than those bacon wrapped cream cheese stuffed peppers we had on the last ski trip. Plus every single girl in our class would see that the person Marcus fantasizes about is me. Oh my gosh, that would be the coolest." Bella is grinning and it's her genuine smile.

"Maybe that's the problem, Bells. You feel the same way about Marcus. Maybe this was just the wakeup call Alex needed to realize we feel differently." My voice comes out heavy and sad. It pops the bubble of Bella's happy little fantasy.

"Then good riddance. I'm coming over after school today. We are going to pig out on something yummy from your kitchen and shop the yearbook for a new crush." She turns toward her next class. "Love ya like a sister, Ems."

"Thanks, Bella." Friends.

Chapter 24

TRUE TO HER word, Bella meets me on the front lawn of the school after last period. We stop at the coffee house for take-out orders on the way to my house. I'm feeling better. There are literally thousands of eligible guys in my area. Why would I waste my time on the blue eyed wonder who ditched me at the coffee house?

"You head for the kitchen and grab us some delicious snack to go with this coffee and I will head right up to your room and find your yearbook. Is it still on the bottom of the bookshelf?" Bella asks as we take our first step onto my driveway.

"It should be. What kind of snack, salty or sweet?"

"Yes." She laughs.

"Alright, deal." The door is unlocked, which means one or more of my parents is home early. If it's Dad we won't even know it. But if it's Mom, our snack choices just got infinitely better. Mom cooks when she is stressed. She also leaves work early when she is stressed. It's not a bad combination for hungry teens.

A peek at the garage finds Dad's car is the one parked. Bummer. I manage to dig up some chocolate chip cookies that look recently baked and half a bag of cheddar potato chips. I'm balancing them, along with my mocha, as I head back toward my room. I should be alright as long as I don't run into anything. The stairs are always the hardest, you have to go very slow since you can't really see your feet.

I'm on the landing, safe, when Dad's office door opens. I jump a little from the shock and have to steady myself. The mocha wobbles dangerously.

"Thanks again, sir. I appreciate all your help."

Is that Tyler? I turn around. Sure enough, Tyler is emerging from Dad's office and they are shaking hands. "What the hell?" I blurt. That earns their attention.

"Tyler came over to discuss some technology things," Dad answers.

"Tyler came over after school to my house to hang out with you?" I ask. My voice drops a little with my sarcasm.

"You mentioned he had questions yesterday. I thought it would be nice of me to answer those for him." Dad claps Tyler on the back in a disgustingly comrade-ish way. "We had a nice chat."

I turn my attention to my friend. Frankly, I feel like I'm more likely to get a straight answer from him. "Ty, how in the world did you beat us here? Did you run?"

"I didn't stop for coffee." He steps closer and takes the mocha from my carefully balanced stack. I relax my shoulders, glad to be able to do that without spilling something. Dad disappears back into the office.

"Want to come up and hang with Bella and I?" I offer. "We were about to consume serious amounts of snacks."

"Lead the way." Tyler smiles.

"Hey Bells, look who I found," I announce, as Tyler follows me into the room.

"Oh, hey Ty. What are you doing here?" she asks. She drops the yearbook she was browsing onto the bedspread and pulls herself up into a sitting position.

"He was meeting with my father." I speak slowly, dropping the words like bombs.

"Shut up. What for?" She turns her shocked expression to Tyler.

"We were just talking. He's a cool guy." Tyler shrugs.

"A cool guy? My Dad?"

"Yeah. He helped to create the chip that everyone has. That's cool, Em." Tyler drops onto the edge of the bed and grabs a cookie.

"Actually, speaking of the chip, I have something else I meant to tell you two." I take a swig of my mocha, building the suspense. "When I was at the office with Carl I saw a strange spreadsheet. It had names of people and dates, which is normal, but it also had names of files that have been uploaded."

"Uploaded? They don't do that. What made you think they were uploaded?" Tyler asks.

"It said file uploaded on the top of the column," I answer. "Anyway, that's not the craziest part." Both sets of eyebrows go up in a weird tandem act. "My name was at the bottom. According to the spreadsheet, file 14.3b was uploaded two days ago. I ran a quick search and that file has never been uploaded before."

"What's a 14.3b?" Bella asks.

"I have no idea."

"You should ask your Dad, he's really smart," Tyler says.

"I did. That brings me to another weird part." I glance over, making sure my door is closed. Part of me wonders if Dad will come up to check on us. Technically, I do have a guy in my room with my door closed. Actually, we're also on my bed together. Plus Dad never actually saw Bella, the buffer. I may not have long before he intrudes on this conversation. I drop my voice to a rushed whisper, "When I was in Dad's office yesterday he was looking over the same file. I figured I better not ask him about it because he obviously already knows. He's being really weird about this whole thing."

"So you didn't ask him?" Tyler asks.

"Technically, no. But he was weird about the letters on the screen. He didn't want to hear anything about how weird you thought that was."

"Wait, what letters?" Tyler asks.

"Seriously, Tyler, what is up with you?" Bella asks, tilting her head like a puppy. "You're all weird today. The green letters that you saw yesterday, remember? The GPS thingies."

"Oh. Well your Dad's probably right about that. I'm sure it's nothing. It's just data everyone's chip records. You'll be ignoring it in no time."

"I'll be ignoring it? That's your new opinion?" I ask. I can't help but remember that was also Dad's opinion.

"Your Dad knows about this stuff, Emma. I think you need to just trust him to handle it."

"Trust him? Isn't that what I've been doing the entire time, Ty? Trusting him and his team to try everything to fix this?" Suddenly I'm angry. I don't need Tyler lecturing me. If I wanted to hear this lecture, I'd go see Dad. I can't exactly take it out on my father, the guy who pays the bills around here. So I take it out on Tyler, hitting him where I know it hurts. "It's like your hero worship thing has kicked into overdrive after you two had a man-to-geek conversation today. I think you should just go home."

I take a deep breath and look apologetically at Bella. "Maybe you both should…"

"I'm sorry, Emma. I was just being honest." Tyler shrugs. "I guess I'll see you tomorrow."

"I'll go too, but call me later," Bella says. She stands up and hugs me.

"Bells, he was being weird, right?"

"Totes weird."

I cross my room and tap the projection plate.

The memory is from yesterday, so it's nice and clear. Bella and I are sitting on the bed. Tyler is standing next to the screen, turned sideways enough so that we can see him. He is squinting at the screen, which is playing the History lesson with the green characters on the bottom.

He looks concerned. He looks worried. He looks frustrated.

"But Em, that doesn't make sense. Your chip wouldn't have any need to recall or record GPS coordinates."

The memory fades and my screen returns to black. I knew it, but I had to see it for myself. Yesterday he was concerned. Today he certainly was not.

What changed?

It sure wasn't the green characters edging the bottom of my screen, those are still glowing strong.

Chapter 25

WHAT IS THE one thing that is guaranteed to take your mind off your stress and complicated life? Vacation. No school, no teachers, no boys. Just me, Bella, and her family traveling to Colorado to ski away four days. It will be beautiful. It will be quiet. It will be peaceful. We will still make it home to eat ham and sing Christmas carols. It'll be perfect.

The lodge comes into view as we turn a windy corner. I love their choice of vacation spot, personally. It's not the largest resort in Colorado, but it's amazing. The lodge is glass fronted and warm. There are other buildings and shops around it, which I hear are even bustling in the summer. They have a large area where people can just sit and hang out in the snow, or I suppose on the grass in warmer months. It makes the last eight hours I spent in the backseat of Bella's family SUV completely worth it.

"I am so glad you made me tag along this year. I love this place. I can feel my excitement building already."

"Me too. What do you want to do first? We could ski," Bella says.

"You girls could just hang out in the lobby with your Mother," Bella's father chimes in from the front seat. He loves taking this annual trip but his wife doesn't ski, which he finds odd. He likes to take every opportunity to throw that into conversation.

Bella's mom turns in her seat. "Oh, you could do that. We can sip hot cocoa and you girls can watch the young boys go by."

"Is that all you girls want to do on your vacation? I'm going to hit the slopes the second we are checked in to the resort," her Dad says. He makes a big show out of throwing the car into park once it's nestled into the spot it will spend the next four days in. "Let's do this." He flings his door open and stretches his entire body as he lifts it from the car. Sure, he looks like a dork, but when you've been driving for eight straight hours stretching feels amazing.

I open my own door and do a similar routine. I'm like a cat, slowly arching each limb to work out the fatigue in my muscles. My legs feel like they are filled with Jell-O. My butt aches. But I don't care, the smile is still plastered to my face.

Bella walks around the car, a similar expression on her face. "I vote skiing. My muscles are too sore for more sitting around."

"Perfect choice," I say.

We all grab luggage, which there seems to be a lot of for only us, and head to the lodge. Bella and I stand off to the side as her parents head to the desk to check us in. They've piled their luggage beside us. Bella is using it to lean on.

"In her odd way, Mom had a great idea," Bella says. "We should be using this opportunity to flirt endlessly with the ski boys around here. It's not like we have anyone at home who would take offense to our flirting, as we're both unattached. Plus the boys and all their strange issues stay right here on the mountain."

Yeah, their strange issues stay here. But what about mine? My malfunction stays with me. That spreadsheet, the one that claims I've had something uploaded, that apparently lives in my house. I wish I could get another look at that spreadsheet. What kinds of files are being uploaded?

I take a step backwards to lean on the wall. The files they're uploading could just be for fixes, like Dad said. The thing that worries me is that he claimed there were never malfunctions before. If there have never been malfunctions, what were the other uploads for?

Bella looks concerned. Her eyes have gone wide. She's looking around me. She reaches out and grabs my arm, pulling me toward her.

"Bells, what the--"

"Oh there it is. Em, you hit the plate." She points to the wall I had just been reclining on. Sure enough, there's a projection plate right there on the wall.

"Where does it project?" I ask. I'm already afraid of her answer.

Bella points again. This time to the huge wall screen in the center of the lobby. The one that is showing an image of the spreadsheet. There are some blurry boxes, the ones I can't remember, but my name is there and the headings are there. "Oh for crying out loud," I moan. I step even further away from the plate and the screen returns to black.

"Don't be upset, Em. No one is ever paying attention to that screen."

"I'm not upset." It's actually true. I'm not. "I'm angry and I'm tired of this crap, but I'm not upset. This is my new normal. Whatever I'm thinking at any given moment could end up being projected to the entire room. I have to stay the hell away from technology."

"You sure sound upset." Bella hangs her head.

"I'm angry. There's a difference. Plus, you don't need to look so sad about it. You've provided me with the best outlet I've had since this all started."

"I have?"

"There's no electronics on a ski slope," I tell her.

Bella's smile returns. "Smarty-pants."

"Guilty." Now we're both smiling.

Bella's parents cross the room with a bellhop in tow. "Alright girls, the room is all set. I'm hitting the slopes," her dad says.

"You're not even going to check out the room first?" Her mom's voice comes out in a whine.

"We'll go with you to see the room and then we're skiing too, Mom," Bella says.

The three of us and the bellhop pile into the elevator. One quick walk around the enormous room later, we're standing in the fresh snow snapping our skis onto our feet.

"This is gonna be great!" I holler over the roar of the wind.

Chapter 26

THE DINNER TABLE is an entirely different atmosphere. Bella and I take our seats, laughing and red-faced from our day outside, to find her parents in a similar state of giddiness. They're holding hands and being generally adorable. Snow is magic.

"How were the slopes, girls?" her mom asks.

"Perfectly refreshing," Bella answers.

The waiter appears out of nowhere, like only waiters and horror movie villains can. He hands us four digital projection menus. This is the fanciest restaurant I've ever eaten in. They have white tablecloths inlaid with gold. The chairs we are sitting in are covered in gold cloths. Tall candles in the center of each table reach toward the ceiling with their sparkling flames. The menus are very small. Each day the lodge serves five signature dishes, no more and no less. The dishes apparently are made with the freshest local ingredients. They use digital menus to make updating them easy. They're thin and light and edged with a protective plastic, but digital nonetheless.

Naturally, I'm nervous to hold mine. I decide to focus on only my menu, nothing else. It can't change its projection if I'm thinking about what it's showing. After a quick read of my options I decide I'm having the beef wellington, for sure. Todd Ramsay is a chef here and his Granddad practically invented the stuff. Well probably not, but he for sure perfected it.

I set the menu on the table. Just as I'm taking my second hand off it, the screen flickers. Oh boy, here we go. I glance around at the rest of the table, they're still looking over the menu. I decide to keep them from seeing anything. I pick the menu back up. Hopefully this isn't a loud interruption. What was I even thinking about? Oh gosh, Todd. His Granddad was a shouter. Let's hope it's a video memory of watching Todd cook on TV and not Gordon.

The screen flickers again. Beef wellington. I just repeat it over and over in my mind. It's making my stomach gurgle in anticipation. Beef wellington. I'm only thinking about the delicious steak, the puff pastry, the sauce. Show me food. I'm hungry.

The screen flickers again. This time I think I see someone before the letters are back. I'm getting warm. I can feel beads of sweat starting on my hairline. I have that urge to scratch my scalp that you get when you start sweating. My leg starts bouncing.

I should put the menu down, but I'm afraid the projection will play anyway. Directed at the ceiling like that everyone would see it. I'm not sure if Bella has filled her parents in on the whole malfunction thing, and I sure don't want to be the person who brings up that awkward topic. If it would just play already I could forget about it.

Like it is accepting my mental command, the screen changes.

Tyler is seated at a table, it looks like we are in the middle of eating. It's a restaurant, I think, although not this one. He's wearing a sweater and his hair is spiked up with gel. An outfit to impress.

"That's what I'm telling you, Emma."

What? Apparently we are mid conversation here. What is he telling me?

"I read about it. Some elderly people begin having memory problems, right? Well your

Dad and the guys over at Neurotech have created these upload files as a sort of memory support training."

The screen flickers a little, but Tyler returns again.

"Your Dad explained it all to me."

I drop the menu on the table and watch it refill with its text. Bella's parents are still whispering quietly, apparently undisturbed by my interruption. Bella, however, is glaring at me from behind her menu. "How the hell did you do that?" she whispers.

"I have no idea." I'm shaking. I can feel it. My hands won't stop their tremors.

"Was that like a fantasy?" Reading my fear, Bella's face changes. Concern starts to crack through her anger; I see it shining out of her eyes.

"No. It looked like a regular memory. Sharp and focused. But it's not   my   memory."

"Did it come from someone else?" she asks.

"No he was talking to me. He used my name."

139

"Okay, so what does that mean?"

"I have no idea. All I know is that Tyler and I have never had the conversation that just played. That memory was not real."

Chapter 27

I SHOULDN'T BE doing this. I shouldn't be standing on Tyler's doorstep on Christmas Eve getting ready to interrupt his family time. But I keep thinking about that odd memory, the one that we never lived, and I need answers.

My hand raises quickly, before I can change my mind, and raps out a beat on the white painted front door. Tyler answers. "Hey Em, what's up? When did you get back?"

"This morning. We need to talk."

"Okay, come on in. Are you okay? You seem worked up."

I push past Tyler into the immaculate living room with the vaulted ceilings that would take a designer's breath away. I shove my right wrist into his face. "You need to tell me everything you know about these chips. Where can we talk?"

"Alright, okay." Tyler throws up his hands. "Let's go to my room."

Tyler's room turns out to be the best place to go. I sit in a big comfy recliner and he drops onto the bed. "I know a lot about those, Em. Let's start with why you're asking."

"Well you know about the malfunction. It's getting worse. When we were at the resort we went to the restaurant, the one with the fancy menu."

"Oh yeah, the daily specials things."

"Yes. Well when I was holding mine, a memory played. But not like a memory. I can't really explain it. I just know that the memory wasn't anything I have lived before. I swear, Ty, it was the weirdest thing. It wasn't like a fantasy image, it was clear and real. Except that it wasn't real."

"Show me." He points to the projection plate in his wall.

I don't want to start a projection. With how things have been going, it's entirely possible something else will come up instead. I walk to the plate like it's going to give me an electric shock. I tap it.

We are seated at the table in a group, Bella beside me and her parents buried in their menus across from me. I'm reading the menu, when it suddenly flickers. I forgot to tell Ty about that part. My indecision on what to do with the menu now comes across as though I'm waving it up and down. The image flickers again. I'm glad the screen isn't showing me, I was probably visibly sweating at this point.

Finally it starts. Tyler at the table in his sweater with spiked hair. "That's what I'm telling you, Emma. I read about it. Some elderly people begin having memory problems, right? Well your Dad and the guys over at Neurotech have created these upload files as a sort of memory support training." Another flicker. "Your Dad explained it all to me."

I step away from the plate, to the safety of the recliner. "I forgot about the screen flashing. That was weird, right? So tell me what's going on."

Tyler stands up, starts pacing his room like a caged animal. "I don't even know where to start. How did you interrupt a static projection? Why did that look like a real memory? What the hell is an upload file, is that like a real thing? What were those green characters on your projection?"

Whoa. At least two of those Tyler should've heard of before. "Okay, I know you're upset, but stay with me here. You knew about the static interruptions, or whatever you call them. Carl found them in his sessions, remember?"

"I didn't know it was working on things like the menu. Those shouldn't even be available to patrons. This is a big deal, Em." He stops his pacing long enough to trap me with a look that makes my stomach flutter. "That memory was fake. Are people manufacturing fake memories now? That's all I could think about while we were watching. Then the fake me uses the word upload, it's blowing my mind." He starts pacing again.

"But Tyler, we've seen that word before. Remember the spreadsheet?" I cross the room again, careful to avoid Tyler on his path, and touch the plate.

The spreadsheet fills the screen. Name, file uploaded, date. A lot of boxes are blurry, since I can't remember them all. But Emma Johnson, 14.3b, December 12 is there.

"This is the best I can recall. There were probably 50 boxes of other names on here." I gesture to the rows above my name. "I vividly

143

remember mine, but no one else's. I did a search for the file name though and there are no other results."

Tyler is squinting at the screen. "File uploaded," he mumbles. He shakes his head and gestures to the bottom of the projection. "And these green things? They were on the bottom of your other memory too. What are they?"

Now I'm getting annoyed. "Tyler, you knew about those. You were the one who told me that they were recording. Then you told me that my Dad probably knew what he was talking about." My voice rises until I'm almost yelling. I take a deep breath, try to calm down.

"But this isn't just a date stamp, this looks like GPS coordinates."

"I know!" Attempts at calming myself clearly didn't work, I'm yelling now. "You already told me that. Ty, what the hell is up with you?"

"We've never had this conversation." He shakes his head.

I can see on his face that he's completely serious. Does he not remember our conversation? I drop my voice a little, take a deep breath. "Tyler, you came to my house and we talked about all of this. You were worried. Then you met with my Dad and--"

"Your Dad? Did he have access to this spreadsheet?"

I'm thrown off by the change in topic. "I think so. For sure Carl had it. Then I think I saw it up when my Dad was working. I'm almost positive."

"Okay." Tyler starts pacing again. I don't know what to say or do so I move back to the recliner and sit down gingerly.

Ty reaches under his bed and pulls a laptop out. This one is seriously old school, gray and boxy. "I want to work on this. You should probably get home before someone notices you're gone."

"Okay, sure." I stand up. "Just be careful, okay? I don't know what is going on lately. Can you catch chip malfunctions? Why are you using that dinosaur anyway?"

"This laptop has no NFC chip. It's completely safe. I use it for hacking."

"You hack?" My eyebrows fly up to my hairline.

"Em, you really should go." Tyler throws me an awkward smile over his shoulder before turning back to the laptop.

I should feel better knowing that Tyler is looking into this. I don't. Instead, I have a whole new thing to be creeped out about. Why is Tyler forgetting things that we already talked about? Why does it seem like his memory loss is directly related to my malfunction?

What the hell is going on?

Chapter 28

"**THE HEART, MAKING** *itself guilty of such secrets, must perforce hold them, until the day when all hidden things shall be revealed.*" The line jumps out at me from the pages of the book. I don't know why that one grabs my attention, but I read it again. Guilt comes from within. I suppose that's a theme of this book. My phone rings from across the room where I've left it. I ignore it, keep reading.

The house phone rings next. The one we never use. The one that is old school. The one I don't know why we have. It's probably someone selling something. I hear the ringing stop, someone must have answered it. I keep reading. The chair I'm curled up in is so comfortable.

"Emma Jean," Mom bellows from the kitchen.

"What?" I match her tone with my own. Slight parts exasperation and annoyance.

"Telephone." I stand up and head to the kitchen where Mom is holding out the old school receiver. "It's Tyler."

I put the phone to my ear. "How did you even have this number?" I ask.

"Let's just say I found it. I have information for you. It's important. Can we meet somewhere?" His voice sounds strange. Clipped.

I try for a casual tone to contrast his whole spy-movie thing. "Sure. Come on over. Mom's cooking something that smells good." My mother shoots me a dirty look, mumbles something under her breath. I catch the word ungrateful.

"No. Meet me somewhere outside."

"What? Why?"

"Just because. How about the park on Bullard; could you get there in a few?"

"Yeah, I guess." The park is bike riding distance, not walking distance. Odd that he wants to meet there. It's not exactly a warm day out. It's like two days after Christmas.

"Thanks. I'm leaving now. See you there." The phone clicks in my ear.

I hang up my end as well. I'm worried. Random rendezvous with Tyler after I asked him to look into my malfunction? What are the odds that this isn't related?

"What time is Tyler coming over?" Mom asks. "He doesn't have food at his house?" She still sounds annoyed.

"Actually, he wants me to meet him at some park. I'm taking my bike. Is that alright?"

"What for?"

"He didn't say," I answer.

"That's weird."

147

"You know Tyler."

Mom takes a second to think. I actually see her shoulders relax and know she will agree before she speaks up. "Alright, that's fine. Should you take a few snacks?"

"Didn't you just mumble something about how ungrateful we are for always taking your snacks?" I ask. There's a hint of teasing in my words.

"Yes, but if you said, "Thank you, Mom, these are the best snacks ever," it would highlight the grateful attitude truly buried underneath."

"Thank you, best Mom ever, for the best snacks ever." I wrap my arms around her waist in a weird she's-cooking-so-we're-backwards kind of hug.

"You're welcome." She hands me an aluminum foil package that still feels warm to the touch. She's been making peanut butter cookies in here and this must be full of them.

My stomach flip-flops. "Oh thank you, for reals. I'm starving." I start to head for the front of the house. "I'll be back later. Love you!"

"Emma, save some cookies for Tyler! And take your phone! I love you, too."

The bike ride takes me almost half an hour. I'm warm from the exertion and the cookies hugging my back through the backpack fabric. But my cheeks feel funny from the cooler air flying past them. I lock my bike to an empty rack nearby. Glancing around the almost empty park, I have to shame myself for that move. It makes it look like I don't trust these people. There's hardly anyone here. Then again, what would I do if someone did steal it? It's not like I'm going to walk the whole distance home.

I cross over to the big trees. This place is cool, it's always been one of our favorite parks. There's a man-made pond thing that they fill with fish twice a year. People can legally fish here, and you often find a few. Today there's a middle aged guy drinking a beer next to a kid who looks like he's sleeping on the ground. Both of them are holding poles, so I guess this is a fishing expedition.

There's also a huge grassy area filled with the kinds of big stately trees that just don't grow naturally around these parts. Then there's the playground for kids and a dog park. On the edge of it all is a large library that I totally love visiting.

The back wall of the library is entirely made of glass windows looking out onto the park. On days when it's too hot or too cold to be out enjoying it, you can curl up in a comfy stuffed chair inside the library and enjoy it anyway. Amazing.

I spot Tyler sitting under a tree and head over. He looks good. He's wearing his hair natural, no gel, just how I always liked it. Maybe this meeting is innocent after all. "Why the bike ride?" I ask, in lieu of a greeting. I flop down on the ground next to him and bring my backpack around to the front, settling it between my crossed legs.

"I didn't think we should talk at your house because of our topic. I did some research and I found some things." Tyler's serious tone makes my stomach drop. Maybe not so innocent then. I'm already sweating from my ride, but if I wasn't before I'm sure I'd start now.

"I got into the company's servers," Tyler says. He drops this fact like a normal person would say 'I tied my shoe,' like it's completely typical. "I was looking for the spreadsheet you mentioned, but no luck."

"It was on a computer Carl uses. Maybe it's not the same since it's old school like yours. Maybe it's not like connected to the network or something."

"Maybe, but I doubt it. Anyway, I found other stuff. I found a file detailing an experiment that was conducted about two years ago. It's like the lab reports we have to write for Science, so it lays out everything about the experiment." Tyler is talking slow like he's headed for something big and doesn't want to rush it.

"Okay." I unzip the backpack and take out the cookies just to give myself a task. Truth is, I'm nervous.

"Basically what I got from the idea of the experiment is that they were trying to upload files and false memories into patients and detail the effects."

"What? Why?" So many questions, but I just can't seem to stop them all wiggling around and grab ahold of one to shove out of my mouth.

"Apparently for this particular trial they selected 50 people. It seems as though their intention was to use themselves and other people with the chip as a control group. These 50 people would have a file uploaded and they would be watched for side effects.

"The experiment was successful, according to them. They called the side effects 'statistically insignificant' toward false memories causing damage to the person. They also concluded that false memories can take roots and become real to the person. They called it 'groundbreaking.' "

"I don't understand any of this. Why would they upload memories? What would be the point of that?"

"Think about it, Emma. They could upload a fake memory of a conversation you had with a presidential candidate. They could make you think you liked what this person had to say. They could make you think he believed what you believed. If you thought you'd personally met this guy and liked him, you'd vote for him. They're trying to control people by manufacturing experiences and memories."

"Who would believe that? Won't they feel fake or look like fantasies?"

"You tell me. You've had one."

The menu. "Oh my gosh, you think that's what that was? You think they're still experimenting? We should tell my Dad. This would prove to him something is being done. He'll know who we should talk to."

Tyler takes a deep breath, lets it out like a sigh. "The trial ended. But yes, I think it's possible that someone kept experimenting. There's something else though. According to the report I found, the 'statistically insignificant' side effect was that 1 of the 50 people studied suffered 'irreparable damage' to their nervous chip."

The little wormy questions are all over the place now. Slippery suckers too. I can't even begin to grab one.

"There's one more thing, Emma." Tyler audibly gulps. I get the impression this is the thing he was trying to avoid. My stomach clenches in anticipation. "The scientists who conducted the trial were Steve Johnson and Carl Simons."

Chapter 29

—◼—–◼—–◼—–◼—–◼—–◼—–◼—–◼—–◼—–◼—–◼—–◼—

"THAT'S IMPOSSIBLE. MY Dad said a chip has never malfunctioned. My Dad always sends me to see Carl, he wouldn't do that if he knew Carl was involved in something like…" The truth is too heavy in my stomach. I hunch over, leaning toward the grass in case I vomit. I stop talking, breathe, and think about the last few weeks. Can this be true? Dad acted weird the moment I asked about my chip. He's been nervous and strange about the green characters. "My Dad is involved." It's not a question now. I can't believe I didn't see it before.

"Do you think you could be that one in fifty whose chip suffered irreparable damage? That would explain a lot," Tyler says.

That would mean, in addition to lying about not knowing what's going on with my chip, my own Dad experimented on me. Could he have created false memories for his own daughter? Uploaded them onto my chip? I shake my head, not because I don't think it's possible, but because I can't process that right now. "I don't remember that at all."

"I think it's safe to say you wouldn't remember it, Emma. We're talking about a company that is manufacturing and uploading false memories. It would be a walk in the park to either erase one or manufacture a new one." Tyler's face communicates total disgust.

Is it possible I sat in that lab once and had Carl sit there and upload other files without my knowledge? I would love to tell you it's not possible, but now I'm not so sure. What would it feel like to have entire days missing? Suddenly, ice begins flowing through my veins as a realization dawns on me. "That's what happened to you. They deleted the memory of our conversation about the green letters."

"What are you talking about?"

"You came over to study history. I put up a video and you noticed those green characters."

Tyler is already shaking his head, "Emma, I didn't see those until you came over the other day."

"Listen to me. I could show you the memory of it--"

"No." The command is loud. I freeze in the act of reaching for my phone and a few birds fly out of the tree overhead. "Emma, if those green characters show GPS coordinates it could be the location you are in when you watch it. I'm not familiar enough with GPS to know whether it's where it was filmed or where it was watched. You can't risk it. Just tell me," Tyler says, his voice back to normal volume.

"Okay, then you have to trust me." I wait for Tyler to nod before continuing. "You told me all about what the letters could represent. You were really concerned. You asked me why I was recording this. I ended up going downstairs and asking Dad about it. I mentioned to him that you even thought it was weird."

"So he knew that I was uncomfortable with it. He probably guessed that I was looking into it."

"When Bella and I came home from school the next day, you were coming out of Dad's office."

"I was?"

"You don't remember that either?" I ask.

"Not really. What were we doing? Did he say?" Tyler looks shocked, but also a little scared. At least I have one of my questions answered. This must be what it would feel like to lose a day.

"Dad said he was just answering a few of your questions. When we all got back up to my room and I brought up the chip subject you were completely different. You kept telling me that my Dad knew best and I should just listen to him. It was so freaky."

"I'm sorry, Em." Tyler hangs his head a little. "You needed me and I must have just let him wipe that memory." He looks so sad. I can't help myself. I lean closer to him, brushing his arm. He practically jumps at my touch. "I wish I could remember what it was like when they did it. I would know what to warn people against. At least then I'd be useful."

"We already know what it's like. You'd never even know it was happening. I sat right there in Carl's office while he uploaded 14.3b and never knew it. You don't feel it and you don't see it." I stroke his arm lightly as I speak, trying to comfort him.

"That may not have been a memory file. We don't know what that was." He turns his brown eyes to me. Tyler has always been a passionate guy, it's one thing I really like about him. Right now his eyes are lit up in an incredibly sexy way. He is fired up about all this, that's for sure. "I think they uploaded some kind of tracer file that time. I think that's what the green characters are."

"So they're tracing my memories?" I ask.

"Maybe."

"They might be able to see this then?" Instinctively I pull my arm away from Tyler. My Dad might be watching!

"I'm not sure how it works. I think they'd probably only see the ones you download to save, send, or recall." Tyler gives me a crooked smile. "It's safe to say based on our topic they'd already be here if they knew."

How did I find myself in this situation? I'm supposed to be a normal high school teenager who hates waking up, loves reading, and has trouble with boys. I'm not supposed to be defined by this stupid chip in my wrist that is malfunctioning. I'm not supposed to find out I'm the girl whose Dad may have volunteered her for some testing that ruined her chip forever. A Dad who then lied to her face about it more than once.

"Are you okay about all this, Emma?"

I don't want to answer him. Instead I scoot my butt closer to him and lean my head on his chest. Reflexively he drapes his arm around my shoulders and pulls my body even closer. I feel safe for the first time in awhile. I close my eyes and let the smell of Tyler just wash over me until my breathing slows down. I can feel Tyler's lips brush the top of my head. His hand traces circles over my lower back.

I pull my head away, just a little, so I can see his face. He offers me a smile. "We're in this together, Emma. We'll figure it out."

I don't think about it. I just lean up and kiss him. Tyler wakes up with the contact and leans into me. I feel the zing of the passion all the way out in my limbs. I keep my eyes closed and enjoy the sensations as Tyler deepens the kiss, winding his tongue around mine.

After the kiss I put my head back on his chest. His heart is speeding away in there. I want life to be like this. Boys and kissing and cuddling in an empty park. I don't want to think about why we are actually here.

Just that quickly I'm thinking about the whole messy situation again. I'm thinking about something Tyler mentioned briefly before he dropped the bomb about Dad. "Do you really think they're still experimenting?"

"Maybe." His voice kind of reverberates in his chest. It makes my cheek feel strange. I sit up but don't move away from him. His arm drops a little, landing on my waist. "The company seems to have known about the experiment. But it has a stop date. Maybe they kyboshed the whole thing, realized it was too dangerous a concept. I would imagine public opinion on this, if it ever got out, would be negative.

"I think it's safe to assume we're dealing with two guys who seem not to care what the company thinks, though. I can't figure out if they are just trying to clean up the mess they made or if they are still making it. That spreadsheet you found might help me get answers."

"It's got to be on Carl's computer. Or Dad's."

"I don't think the computer at your house is the base computer used. It's too new. I think he probably only pulled it up there from memory. I want to see Carl's computer. You described it as being more old school. If they were working outside the confines of company policy, they'd want something older and off network."

"So let's go see that computer," I offer, even though I have no idea how we'd do it.

"We could break into the lab."

I want to laugh at him, because it's a joke. Then I realize he's completely serious. His face is set. This is his best suggestion. "Tyler, I don't think that's a good idea."

"It's a great idea. If we're right about all this then I bet his old school computer doesn't need his NFC chip to activate it. I bet he's got some kind of password I can hack. If we're right about him keeping this from the company then he won't even be able to report the data breach. He'd want to keep all that to himself."

"Wouldn't that make us a target of theirs? Wouldn't they know who was investigating? Last time they thought you were looking into it they wiped memories from your brain, Ty." For a second I actually forget I'm talking about my own father and his friend. They're just scary, faceless men who could come after us.

"Stay near your Mom at all times when you are home."

The mention of home forces the memory back. I live with one of these scary men. The cold fingers of fear tickle up my arms. "Tyler, we have to do something. I'm scared."

"We will. We're gonna break into the lab and get some answers."

Chapter 30

I **PUSH ON** the door, checking to make sure it is securely latched. "They're not even home, Em," Tyler says. "Let's get this done." My projection plate comes to life, presumably at Ty's command. He brings up an image. All black lines on a white background. Too many black lines to make anything out.

I squint a little at it. It looks like the same basic outline shape was used over and over again. "What is this?" I ask, stepping a little closer.

"Blueprints for Neurotech," he answers. "This is the first floor here." He points to the one on the top left. "Then it skips to floor five, because they don't own the first four." His finger moves across the top row.

I skip ahead, counting. "Neurotech owns eight floors?" That seems like a lot to me.

"Apparently," Tyler answers. "You've been there, right? How are we going to enter?" He steps back from the screen and puts his hand on my lower back. He moves me closer to the screen with a gentle push.

I use my fingers to pinch and zoom into the first floor. "You'll go in right here." I point to the entrance along the back of the building, away from the main road. "These are the doors employees use. They enter right into the lobby and the security desk."

"Security desk? How do we get past that?" Tyler asks.

"I'm not really sure. I think it's only manned during business hours when guests can be in the building. There's a key card access panel for employees to use when there isn't someone at security and the doors are locked."

"So we need a key card," Tyler points out.

"I can try and get Dad's."

Tyler rubs my arm. "Are you sure? I don't know how you'd do that without calling attention to what we're doing. That might not be safe. He'd probably notice it was missing. Maybe I should try to connect to the servers and print one."

"That sounds like it would take a lot of time and a special printer. No, I'll just take it. We'll put it back before he even notices it's gone." I sound more confident than I feel. I offer him a smile, hoping it looks genuine. I turn back to the screen. "You want Carl's computer, right? The same one he used on my testing?"

"Yeah," Tyler says from behind me.

"That means we take this bank of elevators up to the seventh floor." I move the screen to floor seven, the last one on the top row on this blueprint. I zoom in to the elevator and then trace the path I walked with Carl to the small room. "Right here." I tap on the small room. "One old school computer, an external connector plate, and a locking door."

"That's our target." Tyler puts a comforting arm on my shoulder.

"It'll work out, Em."

I hear the sound of the front door opening and it makes me jump. "That'll be Dad." Tyler backs away from me and the projection screen goes blank. "Not blank, Ty. That's suspicious. We'd be using it. Put up something, anything," I tell him. I cross the room and open my bedroom door just enough to let in a little light. Having my bedroom door completely closed with Tyler inside would be a red flag for my parents. Having it completely open would be totally out of character. Then I cross back over to my bed and flop down. Tyler has started a video of Math class.

"Why do you have this recorded?" I whisper.

Oddly, Tyler blushes. "I don't remember." He clears his throat. "How are you so sure it's your Dad? Couldn't it be your Mom?"

I shake my head. "Mom would've called out some kind of greeting. Trust me, it's Dad. If he thinks you're here he'll walk by the room and look in. If he doesn't think you're here I may not even see him."

"My bike is out back."

That's right. Parked right on the patio outside the big window. If Dad goes into the kitchen at all, he'll see the bike. I try to look relaxed on the bed. "Well then we better brace for a visitor," I say.

Tyler sits down on the edge of the bed. I scoot my feet over a little to give him space. He's all tense, I can see it in his posture. "Relax," I whisper. "We're just watching Math videos."

I turn my attention to the screen as Tyler's shoulders droop. I'm shocked to see my own face filling the projection Tyler has called up. Tyler sees me like this? I look amazing, radiant. My hair is full and vibrant. My eyes are practically sparkling. I can hear the sound of my own laughter.

The sound of shuffling feet in the hallway draws my attention. I cast my eyes to the right to watch the door without really looking like I'm watching the door. I see a shadow cross the opening. There's a brief knocking and then the door opens, before I have time to even say "Come in."

It's Dad. Standing straight, his shoulders back, looking every bit the master of the household. Somehow, given what I now know, this is past intimidating and firmly into scary. "Hello Emma, Tyler. What are we doing up here?" His eyes skitter to the screen and then to Tyler, where they stay.

"Just watching a Math replay. We have a test." I see the tell-tale blush at his neckline from the weight of the lie.

"I don't particularly like the thought of Emma being up here in her room with a boy when there are no adults home," Dad says, still looking at Tyler. "We have rules here."

"Sure, no problem." Tyler stands up. "I actually have to get home, anyway." He touches my calf, briefly. "I'll see you later." He stands in front of my Dad, holding his own posture straight. "We'll be more careful in the future, sir. Rules are important, after all."

Dad steps out of the way and Tyler leaves. "Emma, you knew the rule. You want to tell me why you thought you could do whatever you wanted?"

There are so many things I want to say right now. Things about doing whatever you wanted with people's memories, about uploading files to your own daughter, about lying. But I need the proof. I grind my teeth to keep the sentences in. "No," I say.

"One week. No one comes over unless we're home. Are we clear?" Somehow he makes it sound like it's not really a question. He doesn't care if we're clear. This is a directive. I nod.

"Good." Dad leaves the door all the way open as he backs out of the room.

I sit on my bed, seething. If we get the proof we're looking for, that makes him the world's biggest hypocrite. Doesn't it? Maybe Tyler is wrong. Maybe Dad isn't involved. Maybe this is all Carl. Maybe Dad was in it in the beginning, but he got out when the company told him to.

I hear the shower start up. Perfect. I push myself off the bed and creep toward my parent's bedroom, peeking around the frame and in the door. There is a shower off of their bedroom. I can see the light pouring out from underneath that closed door. There is no noise from the bedroom door as I push it slowly. Ignoring my pounding heartbeat and my strong desire to run away instead of moving forward, I step into the room. I can see Dad's wallet sitting on his tall black dresser. My ears focus on the sound of the shower as I move my feet. I close my hand on the wallet. No going back now. If that door opens I have no excuse for why I'm standing here with his wallet in my hand.

With that thought, I work quickly. I flip the wallet open and start pulling white cards up. Credit card, grocery store loyalty card. On the third try I hit pay dirt. I put the wallet back exactly where it was and hustle out of the room, pausing long enough to pull the door back to the exact same angle it was left in. I grab my phone and text Tyler.

"I have the keycard. We're good to go for tonight." I sigh to the empty room. The keycard gets shoved into my running shoes and then I stuff those back under my bed. "No backing out now," I whisper.

Chapter 31

WHAT DOES ONE wear to a break in? It's one in the morning. I'm supposed to be throwing on my clothes and taking my bike to meet Tyler down the street. We will drive to the lab, but we don't want to risk starting up a car in either driveway. He's already parked his car at the end of the block. I just need to get dressed. That seems simple, but I have no idea what to wear.

I suppose you should wear black. I own black shirts, but not black pants. How important is the black thing? Is it to keep from being seen? The buildings downtown are all painted in odd desert colors, black will stand out anyway. Shouldn't I wear like brown or beige? Not that I own those.

Alright, this is ridiculous. I should be gone already. I grab a pair of my darkest jeans and pull them on over my sweaty legs. I'm so nervous. Every noise I make is amplified in my head. I keep thinking the sounds will wake my parents, who will come running to check on me and demand to know why I'm awake. Would I have the guts to confront Dad with what I know so far? Tyler seems to think Mom could keep me safe. Do I believe that?

I slip on my sneakers and tie them so I don't trip myself on the stairs. Then I take deliberate steps out of my room, slow enough to ensure there is no extra noise. On the stairs I stay to the right, hugging the wall, where I know they're not as creaky. I decide to skip the last one, since it's been known to groan under my weight, and wipe my brow in victory when I reach the bottom.

The front door will provide a whole other challenge. How do I get out of it without making any noise? It's the thing I've been most worried about with this plan. Tyler can worry about the getting into the computers, I'm just worried about getting out the front door. I take a breath and wrap both my hands around the deadbolt. Maybe my left hand will provide a little muffling. I turn the dial.

There's a clicking. In the silence of the night it sounds like a bomb went off. I freeze.

I count to ten. There's no noise from upstairs. The heater kicks on and I jump. Maybe the heater will provide me a little more cover. I put both hands on the knob now. There's one more dial that has to be turned here. The tiny little locking mechanism seems so innocent. I turn it.

There's another clicking, although not as loud. This time I only count to five when I freeze. Still no new noises. I'm almost home free.

I hold the doorknob tightly in both hands and turn to the right. There's a small noise, but nothing like the first two. I did it! I pull the door towards me. There's a loud kind of sucking noise as the door releases from the frame. I swear it's never done that before. The stupid house is against me!

I wait, silent, standing there letting the cold air in. I think I hear something upstairs. It's now or never, Emma. If they wake up now they may not think to check your room. You're in the clear. If they come downstairs and you're standing here like an idiot dressed in black and holding the door open then the gig is up.

I hustle out the open door, pull it shut, and lock it. All of my motions are a little slower, but there's no pausing at each noise. It's too late for that now.

Chapter 32

"WHERE THE HELL have you been, Em? It's freezing out here."
Tyler is wearing a thick black jacket and a white hat. He's wearing jeans and sneakers just like me. Standing beside the car, Tyler is moving his legs around to keep warm.

"Couldn't you have climbed in the car?"

"I thought it would look strange to see a kid sitting in a car alone at this time of the morning."

"Whatever." I put my bike on the lawn beside his. "We're just leaving these here?" I ask.

"It's the least of our worries, Em." He climbs into the driver's seat of his Mom's Jetta and turns the ignition over. It purrs to life instantly. Her car is in great shape.

I climb into the passenger seat and I'm greeted by blasts of cold air. "Do you have the AC on?" I reach out and flip the vent away from me, toward the window.

"The heat's on, it just takes a second to warm up." Tyler puts the car in gear and pulls out.

There's no one on the road this morning, which is good. I suppose two teenagers in a car after midnight is suspicious. We'd probably get pulled over just for being us. Not like we can have them calling our parents to find out what we're up to. We couldn't exactly talk our way out of it, either. Sorry officer, we just really need to break into this lab and hack some computer to find out what kind of illegal experimentation is going on. In fact, you could follow us. Maybe we'll make a report when we're through. That reminds me. "Hey Ty, what are we gonna do if we find information in there?"

"I don't know. I guess that depends on what they're doing."

"Will we go to the police, turn them both in?" I swallow around the lump in my throat. I'm talking about my father here.

"We have to, Em." Tyler reaches across the center console and takes my hand. "It'll be alright."

I squeeze his hand. "I hope so."

As we approach the tigers that are the buildings Dad works in, I remember the parking lot is badge entry only. "Pull up by that machine," I tell him. I reach into my jacket pocket and pull out the little white card. "Here, swipe this." Tyler looks down at the rectangle with the picture of my Dad's face and smiles at me. It's a sad kind of smile, which perfectly matches how I'm feeling about the fact that I now have possession of that card.

Tyler rolls down the window and swipes it through the machine. The arm jumps up and Tyler rolls into the parking lot. He takes a spot under a tree near the front door of Dad's building.

He holds the card out toward me. "Do you want to hang on to

this?" he asks.

When I turn my eyes down to the card the familiar dimples coupled with the condescending glare from the eyes staring back at me steal the smile right off my face. "No, you hold it." It makes me feel even more guilty just looking at it. I don't know what to make of this new version of my Dad. He's certainly not the guy I thought he was.

Tyler wraps his hand closed around the card. "This card should get us in everywhere, good job snagging it."

We approach the big glass doors with their swipe card access panel on the side. As Tyler walks over to them, I'm almost hoping it doesn't work. It's closer to 2 AM now than 1 AM. I'd rather be in bed, sleeping, than getting ready to unlock whatever secrets are buried inside this building.

The swipe card works. The single door to the left hand side of the three massive glass doors pops open with a loud click. Tyler pulls it the rest of the way and waves me past him.

In the lobby our footsteps echo more than usual. It's unnerving. I'm getting the familiar ball of nerve in my gut, sweat pouring all over my body feeling. I hate that feeling. We cross to the elevators and wait. I'm afraid to look down at the fancy tile for fear that a literal pool of sweat will be there.

The elevator in this building still pumps stupid music into it when no one is here, just in case you were wondering. The doors shut behind us. Tyler is closer to the buttons, so he presses the seven, following the plan we laid out. Meanwhile, I start bouncing on the balls of my feet.

"You're nervous." It's not a question. He knows better than that. Tyler steps closer to me. "I wish I could tell you not to be, but I'm pretty nervous myself. I hope it's going to be alright. Does that help?" He gives me a weak and rather forced kind of smile.

"A little. I like knowing someone is on my side."

"Always." The real smile shines through this time. Tyler bends his head a little, I close my eyes. Tyler and I may have problems, but he has always been a great kisser. His lips are so soft. But this time I don't feel that comforting pressure. The elevator door dings. I open my eyes. "I guess you owe me one. We're here."

Tyler steps off the elevator with me right behind him. I step around him and lead the way back to the room where Carl performed some odd tests on my chip and possibly uploaded some strange file.

The chairs are still there, the computer still on the table. I can see them through the tiny window beside the door. The one that's locked. "I guess I didn't think it would be locked. I'm sorry."

"Don't be." Tyler swipes the badge again. The door opens. "Your Dad has access."

Just like that, we're in. Tyler drops down into Carl's chair and powers up the tower we came here for. Me? I'm frozen in the doorway. Beyond that door my Dad could be involved in something big. Right here in the doorway, I'm safe. I can't seem to step in.

"I'm gonna try a few things for Carl's password first, but there's an icon for your Dad. If I can't hack the password in two tries you'll have to try your Dad's. Okay?" Tyler starts typing. He doesn't really need my answer to start his plan.

Clicking. Sigh. Clicking. "Shit. Emma, what's your Dad's password?" Now I have his full attention. His eyes take in my panicked expression, my calves taut from standing on my toes, my generally ready for flight attitude. "Em, it's okay. We just need this file. Maybe I can even remove whatever they uploaded if I know what it is."

"Try Hannah23, no spaces, capital H." It barely comes out of my mouth. It's his password at home, I want to explain. It's how old my Mom was when they got married. Dad says it's the age his Hannah was when she changed him for the better. Was he lying about that, too?

"You're brilliant, Em! I'm in." The clicking picks up speed. I'm tempted to turn around and head back to the lobby. Is it too late to claim I had nothing to do with this?

The clicking stops. "Em, you have to either leave or focus. I can't work if you take control." Tyler turns the screen toward me, where it's filled with an image of my house in what appears to be a monsoon storm. Water is pouring out of every opening.

"I wasn't thinking about that." Like the rotten kid in class being caught by a teacher, the screen returns to what Tyler was trying to do. I step into the room. Seeing that little blip, the one I didn't even know I was thinking, reminded me why I'm here. Someone has hacked my head. "Let's do this." I pull the other chair over beside Tyler and sit.

Tyler is seriously impressive with a computer. He types quickly. I can't keep up with all the files he's opening and closing. I never really thought of computer skills as a superpower before, but I'm starting to now. Still, an excessive amount of time has passed with no results. We absolutely have to leave here by 4:15 to be home before my Dad wakes up. It's now 3:02. "Tyler, are you sure--"

"Got something. Does this look familiar?" A spreadsheet fills the screen. My eyes roam over the screen, taking it all in.

"Scroll down." I'm talking to Tyler, but it scrolls on its own.

"Or you can." Tyler smiles.

"That's the one. See. What the hell is 14.3b?"

Tyler clicks around inside the folder that produced the spreadsheet. He finds a ton of information. There's the start of an official document that looks like another experiment log. Tyler is right, it looks like the lab reports we hate to write for Science class. There's a list of participants. There's a memo from the department explaining that all upload experimentation is to be halted effective immediately. That one is dated January 1st.

"That spreadsheet must be what they switched to after the January first ruling. Notice the first entry is January 2? These aren't people the company knew about," Tyler says.

"So what are they uploading?"

"I don't know. There's a few more documents here though." He clicks on and is rewarded with our answers. This is a list of file names and upload descriptions. We are both silent as he does a search for 14.3b.

Tears spring to my eyes. "Tracker file. You were right, they're tracking me."

"Maybe it's just Carl, we don't know." Tyler brushes my hand.

"You're logged in as my Dad. Plus, I remember them talking beforehand. Carl asked him if he was still okay with this upload. He said yes." I swallow hard. "Can you take it out?"

"Um..." Tyler trails off as he starts clicking more things. "It doesn't look like it, Em. I don't know it well enough. But once this all comes out, someone will be able to. There's one more file in here I want to look at, then we can go." Tyler clicks on the last file.

It's a video. It's grey and blurry, like nothing I've ever seen before. It sort of looks like my school, but in a weird way. Almost like someone took a gray and white watercolor painting of my school and starting dripping water down it, slowly ruining the image.

A creepy shapeless blob enters the screen from each side. "Emma, did you hear about the news?" The monotone computer sounding voice comes from the one on the right.

"It turns out someone hacked the lab and uploaded a joke file using the names of real patients." The one on the left speaks in the exact same monotone.

"So this was all for nothing. We didn't need to panic."

"What the hell was that?" I ask.

"I think we just found out what the uploaded memories look like before upload. I bet your brain fills in all the rest of the details. Those shapeless blobs would probably become me and Bella."

"So it would look like our school?" I ask.

He shakes his head. He is angry. I can see his jaw working, he is grinding his teeth. "This is sick."

"What are you gonna do now?"

"I'm going to save this entire folder to a USB stick. I'm taking it to the cops tomorrow." He looks over his shoulder to see if I have any objections.

After seeing that video, I don't. These people are intentionally playing with our minds. Fuck them. "Okay."

At my permission, Tyler turns back to the computer. He plugs a skinny stick thing into the tower, clicks a few buttons, and waits. The screen shows the background and a progress bar, nothing else. "What is that thing, anyway?" I ask, pointing to the stick.

"It's called a USB, it's like a tiny hard drive. It holds information."

"Oh. So all the files will be on there and not on this tower thing?"

"Actually, that's a great idea, Em." The progress bar fills all the way and closes. Tyler finds the folder and reopens it. He selects everything in it. "This should piss them off." He clicks delete. "Now the folder is empty." I watch as clicks something that brings up a box. More clicking shows me a screen where he is selecting a disk. "And as soon as this defrag finishes running, I'll be the only person who has all this information."

"Let's take it to the police station. Right now, before they do anything else," I tell him. Yes, I'm aware I'm talking about my own father. I just don't care.

Chapter 33

THE ELEVATOR DOORS open, showing us the empty lobby. I step out first and start walking toward the entrance doors. At the security desk, I pause. "Was this there when we came in?" I ask. I point at the security desk where a mug sits center table in front of a rolling chair.

Tyler reaches around me and lays his hand on the mug. "It's warm," he says.

"Where do you think this person is now?" My voice drops to a panicked whisper. We have no reason to be here, a stolen keycard is in my pocket, and a flash drive full of information we shouldn't have in Tyler's. This is not good.

"Well, whoever poured this coffee isn't standing here right now. Let's get out of here." Tyler heads to the door. He looks both ways like a studious boy scout before crossing the street and then pushes the door open. I jog to follow him. The cold air slaps me in the face and I pull my jacket closer around my body.

There's no sounds or signs of anyone. We walk quickly. Being out of the building is comforting. You can't prove we were breaking and entering if we're outside, right? Oh, God. We were breaking and entering. My pulse is skipping around in my wrists and my neck so strong that I feel it like the bass of a song turned up too high.

At the edge of the building, Tyler stops. He puts up a hand to stop me as well. He leans forward, peeking around the corner. I lean to the right, checking the parking lot. My blood runs cold and I smack Tyler, hard. He squints at me, the unasked question clear in his eyes. He wants to know what that was for. I point.

There's a white pickup truck with an orange flashing light bar on top of the cab driving slowly around the parking lot. The word "SECURITY" is painted on the door. He's at the second to last row of cars, heading away from us. I hold my breath as I watch the truck come to the end of the row. He turns to the right, to the final row. Now he's coming directly at us.

"He's almost done," Tyler says.

"What do you think he does when he is done?" I ask, my voice too high because of the stress.

"I assume he'll head back in for his coffee. We need to move."

The truck finishes the final row and turns left out of the parking lot. Something occurs to me. "I've never seen that truck before. They must park it somewhere out of sight." That could be good for us. Out of sight means we may have a chance to get into the car.

Sure enough, the truck heads out of my vision toward a little building across from this one. Maybe it's a parking garage. I don't know. Honestly, I don't really care.

Tyler and I take off, jogging to the car. I jump into the passenger seat and shut the door just as he fires up the engine. He must be as nervous as me because I'm sure he leaves streaks of the rubber from his tires on that parking lot. Looking behind us I see the old security guard who works the desk walking across the path that leads up to Neurotech.

The worst part? I'm pretty sure he's focused on us, too.

Chapter 34

THE INSIDE OF the police station looks nothing like I would've imagined. For one thing, the floor is a polished white. In the movies isn't it always like a brown carpet that gives the entire place kind of a grimy, dirty feeling? In real life there is a sweet looking lady cop sitting behind a desk up front and it's rather quiet. She is typing away at something and we can hear every click.

Tyler steps up to the counter. "We need to speak with a detective." He nervously fingers the USB stick in his right pocket.

"What for?" she asks.

"We have information about a crime," he answers.

"Is that an open crime? One we would already be investigating or that you heard about on a tip line?"

"No. It's one we need to report, like open a file on."

Besides wouldn't we have just called the tip line if your way made sense?

"Alright," she says, "let me just see if anyone is available. Go ahead and come around." The door to her right buzzes a little as it unlocks.

Tyler pulls the door open and we follow her into a large room. It's not quite full like the movies would have you believe, desks everywhere and policemen scattered around working hard. There are about five desks and only one is occupied. Everything is clean and orderly and it smells like coffee. The female cop gestures to an empty desk on our right. "I think your best bet would be to wait here for Martinez. I'll go grab him. You two can have a seat."

We both flop into the two chairs in front of the desk that must belong to Martinez, whoever he is. When the lady cop walks away, I turn to Tyler. "Are you sure about this?"

"I was about to ask you the same question." He chuckles.

"I'm okay, I think. Just nervous." My leg starts bouncing as if to prove my statement.

Obviously Tyler is the same. He has taken his hand out of his pants pocket so he can sit comfortably, but now the hand is protectively sitting on top of the USB stick. He looks like he is in the middle of tapping some rhythm on his leg, forever frozen waiting for the next beat.

"How long do you think we'll have to wait here?" I ask.

"I have no idea, I've never been here before."

"It doesn't look like I pictured."

"I think I was expecting old school computers to be propped up on big wooden desks. Maybe be full of guys in button down white shirts," Tyler agrees.

I chuckle a little. "Sleeves on their shirts rolled up to their elbows and suspenders too?"

"That would be closer to what I was picturing, yeah. This is like any old office building, almost."

"Well I don't know that I've ever seen an office building that crams five desks into one area like this."

"True, I'll give you that," he smiles. "Hey, thanks for coming with me. I was afraid you wouldn't."

"I think I have to do this, Ty. I'm so angry at him for what we found."

"I know."

Now we're back to the present, to why we are here. I can tell he is thinking about how heavy this is too. He's moving his thumb like he is making sure the USB stick hasn't gone anywhere.

We both jump when the door from the reception area opens again. I look over Tyler's shoulder and see the same lady cop coming through. "Espinoza is just through here, he was expecting you."

So, clearly, whomever is coming through the door is here to report a crime. It's not Martinez. I turn back toward the desk.

"Thank you."

The voice is familiar. I turn a little, trying to place where I have heard that voice before. My eyes widen as I take in the man, belly bulging underneath a blue button down shirt. The logo over the pocket, the name tag clipped above that.

"What's wrong?" Tyler whispers.

"We have to go." I can't give him more than that. Not now. We just have to get out of here, quick. Before something goes wrong. I stand up and walk to the lady cop, who is returning to her locking door. "We have to go. My sister just texted me that we have kind of a family emergency."

"Would you like to leave a statement or some evidence for

someone? At least leave your contact information."

"We will be back, actually."

"Oh, okay. Well let me at least get you Martinez's card." She opens the door and bends down behind the desk. I stand nearby, watching and bouncing on my toes. Tyler takes the card when it is offered.

I have never dashed out of a building so fast in my life. I don't even stop until I'm buckled into the passenger seat of the car. Tyler takes his time opening the driver door, sitting, and starting the car. His jaw is clenched and he's refusing to look at me. On the steering wheel, his knuckles are capped with white spots. He pulls out into traffic before he speaks. "You want to tell me what the hell just happened? You don't even have a sister."

"That guy who came in to report a crime with Espinoza? He is the security guard at Neurotech. It's the same guy who was driving that truck this morning."

"Wait, seriously?"

"Yes. I've met him before. He stands at the desk and makes everyone sign in if they are not a badge carrying employee. Tyler, he was there to report the break-in. What were we thinking? They have to have security cameras there. It would be as easy as flipping on the screen and checking to see that, although it was his card, it was definitely not Steve Johnson entering at that time. We could be charged with all kinds of things."

"Okay, wait. Calm down. You didn't hear him say he was reporting a break in. Why wouldn't he call a detective to come to Neurotech if it were to investigate a break in?"

"I don't know. Why would he be at the police station the day of a break in if not to report a break in?"

"It didn't even look like a break-in. Unless someone, like your Dad, decided to tell them that the files had been wiped off the computer, he wouldn't know anything."

"But if someone did report it then he can probably find video of it."

"Do you want me to lie to you?"

I'm taken aback a little by the question. "What? No, why would I want that?"

"Then, yes. The answer is if he went looking there is probably video of us entering. There is a little camera in the lobby. Honestly they probably won't look at the video unless someone suspects something. I told you, I don't think Carl or Steve would report the missing files. Besides, we were there to hand them the missing files. I just think you overreacted."

Did I? I just saw that security guard and... "I panicked, Ty."

"I saw that."

"Maybe I wasn't quite as ready for this as I thought." He doesn't answer. I suppose he doesn't really have to. It's pretty obvious that I'm right about that one. "What do we do now?"

"Let's put your mind at ease about this whole thing. I'll take you home. You'll spend the day relaxing and catching up on sleep, but be awake when Steve comes home from work. Eavesdrop if you have to, from a safe distance. Find out if he is nervous about anything, if he suspects anything, if he reported anything. Let me know. Then we will proceed with our police plan when you are feeling a little more comfortable. Deal?"

What do I say to that? "Yeah, I guess."

"Emma, we need to report this. It's not going away. What they are doing is wrong."

"I know."

Tyler stops the car at a red light on Grand Avenue, meaning we probably have more than five minutes to sit and talk safely before this light changes, and that's if there's no train today. He turns toward me. "I'm serious. I know Steve is your Dad and I know this is hard for you, but these files prove that things he is doing are straight-up wrong. I have to tell someone. We have to keep him from taking this little experiment further. I'll go without you if I have to."

"You don't have to. I'll be okay, but give me a little more time."

"I am." He checks to make sure the light is still red then leans closer and kisses me on the cheek. "I'm sorry we have to do this."

"I am too." I want to say that I appreciate him being there with me, in this awful situation. I want to tell him that I never imagined I would drag my friend along into a nightmare like this. The words are trapped in my throat. Instead, I reach out and turn on the radio. I let the sounds of the bands fill the car and we ride home without saying another word.

Chapter 35

—-■-—-—■-—-—■-—-—■-—-—■-—-—■-—-—■-—-—■-—-—■-—-—■-—-—■--

"Wow, Em." **Bella** has been officially brought into the loop. This is her breathy reaction.

"Right? I think I was hoping we'd find something that incriminated Carl and not Dad. I wasn't expecting to find it all while we were logged in as Dad. I mean, that really means he's been doing this. The company told them to stop and they didn't."

"It's about the science. They must have thought the results they were going to get were more important than the people affected."

"I guess that's the part that hurts. He thought that even when it was his own daughter."

"I'm so sorry. It's not even enough to say that, is it? How do you express the pain I'm feeling for you in words?"

"I think you just did."

"Well good, because better words are completely failing me right now."

Where I'm sitting, near a window in my living room, I can clearly see the street. A familiar black Lexus turns left, making its way to our house. "Hey Bells, I have to go. I see my Dad's car coming."

"Shit, okay. Hey, be safe please."

"Will do. Bye." I hang up before she can say anything else, slide my phone in between the cushions on the couch, and grab the book on the table beside me. I have to look busy and disinterested.

I have never before noticed how long it takes my father to drive down our street, park the car in the garage, and come inside. I'm nervous and seriously fighting an urge to bounce my leg. I pull it up into the chair underneath myself, using my weight to stop it.

I hear the door open, the keys get tossed onto the counter, footsteps crossing the kitchen. Mom would be calling out a greeting right now. Dad is silent. Is that because he has always been silent when he comes home, or is he stewing in his anger about the break-in? My heart speeds up. I hear some noises; maybe the fridge and a cabinet being opened. Getting a drink, maybe? I hear the sound of something being poured into a glass. That refreshed sigh that follows up a gulp of something cold. Do you get a drink if you have video evidence of your teenage daughter essentially breaking into your lab? Do you stand in the kitchen relaxed and having a sip of tea while your security guard turns over evidence to the police department?

He saunters into the living room. "Hi, Emma."

That sounded normal. "Hi," I answer. My own voice sounds more hesitant.

"I'm gonna go for a run around the block, you coming?" he asks.

Seriously? "No, I'm just gonna stay here."

"Suit yourself." Dad heads off to his room, presumably to change into something more running appropriate than a button up white shirt and a silk tie.

Should I take this as a good sign that he knows nothing about our rendezvous? His face showed none of the stress I would expect from someone who tried to access a file that was deleted from his computer. Certainly none of the panic or anger from someone who has already seen the video of the people who were responsible.

He emerges back into the living room in a pair of gray shorts, a yellow dry fit shirt, and a pair of jogging sneakers. "Sure you won't come along? Good for the muscles."

"No, I'm good. Dad, how was work?"

"It was work, Emma. Same old, same old."   He frowns at me. "Why?"

"Just curious."

"I'll be back in a bit."

I watch him jog off down the road until he turns the corner and disappears out of sight. Then I fish my phone out of the chair. *Call Tyler,* I think. Tyler's picture and the green calling banner fill the screen.

"Hello."

"Hey, it's me. Dad just came home."

"And?"

"He seemed normal, I guess. He's gone out for a jog right now," I say.

"Does he normally do that?"

"Sometimes. I asked him about work though and he just said it was work. Didn't give me any details."

"That's because he probably doesn't know any details, Em."

"I'll feel better once Mom comes home. He talks to her about his day all the time. I'll get more information then."

"Okay."

I can hear it in his voice. Tyler doesn't think there's more to get. He thinks I'm overreacting. I can only hope he's right.

Chapter 36

"**HOW WAS WORK?**" Mom asks. My parents are standing over the kitchen sink, washing dishes in tandem. They do this a lot. It's kind of adorable. I am sitting in the living room, on the floor, with my back to the wall. I can hear everything they are saying, but I'll have a really hard time explaining why I'm there if either one of them questions it. We've all just finished up dinner. No one really talked during dinner, although that isn't unusual.

"It was alright," Dad answers. "We finished up that experiment we were working on and sent the results into corporate. Now we just wait."

"You seem a little stressed."

"No, I just hate waiting for their approval on everything I do. Don't they pay me to do this work? They should just trust that I have done it and done it well."

I roll my eyes, glad they can't see.

"It's the same way in every job, Steve. I have other judges who sit in on my cases from time to time to perform peer reviews. Today someone even took my files on a case and sifted through it with me. It's good, sometimes, to bounce ideas off other people."

Yeah, but not when you're hiding something major from those other people, Mom. Of course, I can't really explain this to her and I know Dad won't. Guilt starts to knot my stomach. I just want this to be over. I should've turned it over to the police today when I had the chance.

"Speaking of court, how was the case today?" Dad asks.

"You know I can't talk about it. It's going to be a long one."

"I heard a tidbit about it on the news, something to do with robbery?"

"Yes." She won't tell him more than that. I wonder how much he will push before she gets angry. I've seen her storm off and slam doors because he wanted to know about cases before.

"There was a robbery at work, actually. Not that it's related to your case," Dad says.

My breathing stops. Any movements I was making stop. That heavy feeling like cement is flowing through my veins takes over. I couldn't move right now if I wanted to.

"Oh yeah?" Mom asks.

"Our security guard, Tom, had his kid's bike stolen out of the back of his pickup truck on the lot."

"When did that happen?"

"Well the bike was gone when he went out to put something in his car right after he got to work this morning. He knows it was in the car when he left home. He didn't really notice one way or the other when he pulled into the lot. He's always the first one at work, so no one can vouch for when it went missing. He had to go up and file a police report today."

"Maybe it will turn up."

"I think the company will probably take up a donation to buy a new one for the kid either way," Dad says.

I let out the breath I was holding slowly, pursing my lips and blowing the air out like a I'm extinguishing a candle. They don't know anything.

"You should donate at least a little something."

"I think I will."

I push myself off the floor and head for my room. On my way past our low, wooden coffee table I bend at the knees so I can grab my phone. *Call Tyler.* I command. Again, the green line lights up below his picture.

"Hello."

"Are you still mad at me?" I ask.

There's a small chuckle. "I was never really mad. I just want this to be in the hands of the people who can take it to the next level, Em."

"Well, he doesn't know anything. You were right."

"I know. At least, I suspected. I've been watching the news off and on all day. I have a feeling they would've at least mentioned a break in at Neurotech if one were reported."

"Apparently the security guard was reporting a bike that was stolen out of his truck. Get this though, my Dad submitted some other results to his bosses today. You don't think it's related, do you?" I ask.

Tyler is quiet for a moment while he thinks. "No. One, I don't think they know this experimenting is still going on and I'm pretty sure he doesn't want them to. Two, we have their files. They could recreate a lot of it by uploading memories, but we have the originals."

"Three," I add, "he seemed irritated with the entire process. I don't think he likes having someone approve his research."

"That matches with what I was thinking as well. Geeze, Em, this

189

is such a mess. I'm so sorry."

What do I say to that? I knew my Dad and I had issues, but I didn't realize what a monster he really was. He knows what he is doing over there, he has to. Yet he keeps doing it. In the name of what? Science? Mind control? "Hey, I'm gonna go get some sleep."

"You want me to come by?" Ty offers.

"No, I'm okay here. I'll call you tomorrow."

"Okay, bye."

I hang up with Tyler and throw my phone on the charging pad next to the bed. Then I flop all my weight onto the mattress and stare up at the ceiling. My father is uploading false memories to the nervous system chips of people, including me and Tyler. He is altering memory for the purposes of controlling their minds. There is no good excuse for that.

Text Tyler, "Go to the police station tomorrow. Don't let me talk you out of it." I command. I hear the little whoosh sound that accompanies a sent text and sigh.

There's a ding of an incoming text. I reach out my right hand without looking and grab the phone. I don't turn my head, I bring the screen directly in front of me and hit the button to read the text. It's from Tyler.

"I was already planning on it."

Everyone needs friends like these.

Chapter 37

"**SO THAT'S WHAT** happened. Ty is waiting until they open the station at 8 AM and then he's going down there to hand everything over to the police." I'm on my cell phone with Bella. It's still dark in my room, but my phone thought it would dial Bella's number for me. Nice of it. Anyway, I think I've caught her up on the new developments.

I let the comment hang there in the room for a minute before I go on. "I have to talk to him. I want to give him a chance to tell me something that makes me feel better."

"Like to defend what he did? Emma, I'm not sure there was a better reason he's going to give you."

"I know, but I want to try. It's my Dad, Bells."

"Alright, well Ty is going to the police one way or the other in twenty minutes. Go downstairs and talk to him, I guess. What could it hurt?"

"I think I will. Thanks."

"Anytime. Although next time I'd prefer it if you just take me with you."

"I sincerely hope there won't be a next time," I answer. "Talk to you later."

Hanging up, I know she's right. I can't stop Tyler now, and I really don't want to. But I can talk to my father. Odds are this won't end up like some old-timey TV show where the Dad has all the answers and wraps you in a hug that makes everything sunny again. Let's face it, we're not that family. But maybe he'll have an answer that makes the knot in my stomach loosen just a little.

In the kitchen I find both my parents sitting around the table. Mom has a steaming mug in front of her and the newspaper open. Dad has a plate that holds the remnants of scrambled eggs and is working on a bowl of fruit. I stand in the doorway, looking serious and taking deep breaths, until they both look up.

"What's up Emma-Jean? Are you alright?" Mom asks.

"I'm tired."

Dad looks back down at his plate like we've lost his interest. I glare at him. "I haven't really been sleeping well since I saw a bunch of stuff on Carl's computer over at the lab."

That earns his attention. The wooden chair scrapes across the linoleum as he jumps to his feet. "You what?"

"Tyler and I used your swipe card and went into the lab." I lob the card across the table like a Frisbee. It lands in the center of the table, the face of the monster who thought it was alright to upload fake memories to people staring up at my ceiling. Mom glances down at it before looking back to us, watching the confusing tennis match.

"That's a nice confession, Emma. Will you be telling that to the police who investigate our break in?" Dad asks. He doesn't even sound like himself. Venom is dripping from his words. Somehow that makes what I'm about to say easier.

"I'll be telling it to the police, but they'll be investigating something else. Tyler has all the proof he needs. We know what you've been doing, Dad. Even better, we can prove it. I just came down here to ask you why you did it. I'm hoping you'll give me something that makes me feel better."

"What is she talking about, Steve?" Mom looks concerned. She should be. Sorry about the coming world-shattering, Mom.

I keep my attention focused on Mom to avoid looking at Dad. I let it all out of the bottle. "Dad and Carl have been manufacturing and uploading fake memories to people. In the beginning, the company knew about it. They ran a study of 50 people. After one of the 50 people suffered irreparable damage to their nervous chip, the study was discontinued. It was deemed unsafe. But Dad and Carl had to keep going. They uploaded more fake memories. They're playing God over there in that lab." It feels good to get that all out. I turn my attention back to Dad. His face has gone red. "Is that about right, Pops?"

"What proof could you have?" Even as he asks it, I can see he realizes the answer. I wouldn't know all this without documents. I already told him I was in the lab. "You have the spreadsheet." It's a fact, not a question. Dad's a smart guy.

"We have the spreadsheet, the list of people who had uploads after the trial stopped, all the information about the trial, and one fake memory recently created but not used yet."

"You've actually seen one of these fake memories, baby?" Mom asks.

"Yes. Tyler and I watched one that was obviously intended for

193

me."

Now it's Mom's turn to scrape that chair across the floor. But when Mom does it, it's a deliberate act and it takes longer. She scrapes it slowly like the crescendoing music when the bad guy is about to arrive on scene. She stands up from it at the same pace. Once she is fully erect she glares across the table at my father. "You intended to upload a memory to alter our daughter?"

"Uh, Mom. I hate to break this to you but Tyler and I are pretty sure I may have been the 1 in 50. It would explain the whole chip malfunction thing. Plus we already know he uploaded a tracking device to my videos and uploaded a fake memory to both Tyler and I. I think it worked better for Tyler than me. Maybe because of the damage to my chip, I don't know."

I think, up until the moment I told her that, my Mother could've forgiven him. Something breaks in her expression when she hears my friend and I were involved. Something just got personal. She crosses her arms over her chest and gives him her judge stare. "You have 2 minutes to state your case," she says, all business.

"We needed a child for the original testing. I couldn't tell you because you wouldn't understand. I brought Emma into work with me. The memory we uploaded was of her playing in my lab all day, even though she only sat around in a room. I felt guilty, but we needed to analyze her results."

I remember that day. The funny thing is, I've always thought I went two days in a row. I remember a boring day sitting in a room with a book and nothing else. Dad didn't even sit with me, I was so bored. Then I remember a day where Dad and I ate in the cafeteria and I got to see his lab. They were so different but I do remember them both. Was the second one completely fake?

"Something went wrong, obviously. It's like Emma's chip wouldn't take the data. She, even as a child, knew it was a false memory. It caused damage, but we couldn't tell how much. The company ran a few tests, but it didn't seem to affect her memory. They labeled it as irreparable only so they had an excuse to stop the testing."

"When was this?" Mom asks.

"It would've been about two years ago," I answer. "I wouldn't exactly call myself a kid, Dad. If you noticed other problems or my chip started messing up, why didn't you just immediately bring me back up to the lab for some testing? I was obviously a subject they knew about." The first time, anyway.

"We had to keep it isolated. If we told the company they'd stop the rest of the testing. You have to understand, Emma. One person having side effects shouldn't be a deal breaker. This is a stupid policy. We've uploaded memories of all sizes and all importance to over one hundred people. You are the only one who has suffered damage. The only one. That's one percent, Emma. That's better results than any other scientific trial of our time." Dad is starting to get really animated, using his hands to gesture. Talking about science fires him up.

"We have proven we can alter the memories of a human being with ninety-nine percent accuracy, Emma. Do you understand what that means for the future?"

I think he expects me to get excited. To join him in some chest-smacking, ball-spiking display of success. Instead, I meet his gaze. "Yes. It means you and your buddies are messing with people's minds. It means brainwashing." I work as much venom into that one word as I can. "It means being able to control ninety-nine percent of the population is more important to you than your own daughter." It hurts. That ball of regret that has been in my gut just exploded and sent shrapnel straight for my heart. I reach up to brush a strand of hair out of my face and realize I'm crying. I don't know when I started that, but it makes sense. Once I know I'm crying, I only cry harder.

Mom walks across the room and wraps me in a hug. We drop to the floor that way, me cradled in her arms. She looks over my head. "I think you should go," she says. Dad doesn't argue. He just walks out of the kitchen.

"I'm so sorry, baby. I don't know what else to say." Mom kind of coos into my hair as she holds me. I let her do it. I let her treat me like a baby. It feels safe and it feels warm.

Mom and I both look up as the sound of crashing emanates from the hallway. Another noise and I stand up. Mom joins me and we both watch the doorway. "It sounds like it's coming from Dad's office." I'm sure she knew that too but I feel more helpful saying something.

"Do you have plenty of evidence even if he were to trash that place? Could he be looking for something important?"

I reach out and take her hand. It's trembling. My strong mother, the judge who knows that this has to end in his arrest and possible conviction, is scared. She's playing tough for me. I don't have words enough to tell you how that feels; I want her to be able to fall apart. I pull my shoulders up and put on a brave face. "We have enough, Mom."

"Good, then he can do whatever he'd like in that room."

Together, we step out into the living room. I think we both want to watch him leave the house. The banging stops. Dad emerges from the office into the hallway. He has put on a black hoodie, jeans, and running shoes. There's a bag slung over his shoulder. As he catalogs our appearance he jams a black hat onto his head. He looks like a completely different person. Turning his eyes away from us, Dad slowly starts walking toward the front door.

I smell it before I see it. Smoke. Thick, black smoke. It pours out of Dad's office, engulfing the hallway before he even reaches the door. Mom drops my hand. She heads toward the office. I head toward Dad. What has he done?

I reach the door before he does and throw myself flat against it. "What did you do?"

"Get out of the way, Emma Jean."

"Did you start a fire? What the hell were you thinking?"

"Emma, get out of my way. We all need to get out of the house."

"Answer me and I'll move!" I don't feel this brave. I'm shaking from head to toe. I'm not sure what's keeping me here.

Mom appears in my line of sight again. "Emma, open the door. We need to get out. I can't find the fire extinguisher." She pulls a cell phone out of her pocket and dials 9-1-1.

Dad lays his hands on my right arm and yanks with everything he has. He is stronger than I thought. I travel pretty far. After he lets go, I lose my balance and fall hard on my side. My arm hurts, my side hurts, even my leg hurts. I watch as he wrenches the door open and takes off running.

Mom reaches me, pulls me gently to my feet, and we run out to the cool air. Both of us take deep breaths and watch the smoke pour out of the front window for the office. My eyes start scanning the front yard. When it's empty I turn my head and body to scan both sides of the street. "Damn it, I don't see him anywhere. He was just here. Where did he go?"

"His car is in the garage, so wherever he went, he walked." Mom slips her arm around my shoulders. It actually hurts when she touches my right arm on the far side. I wince. "The police will be here soon, they'll find him."

Police cars, ambulances, and fire trucks surround my house. In no time at all, I'm sitting on a stretcher bound for the hospital while Mom sends the police out to search for the arsonist who burned our house.

No one has anything to say when it just happens to be her husband.

Chapter 38

"**WE GO LIVE** now to the scene at Neurotech, where a recent discovery brings the near ubiquitous Neurotech chips into question. Gina?" I reach for the stupid stick that controls my hospital bed and the TV. I hit what I hope is the volume up button.

The news anchor desk fades to a perky blonde in a blue blazer. "Thank you, Kim. I'm live here at Neurotech where Carl Simons, one of the two men credited with helping to create the chip everyone wears in their arms, has been arrested. The charges are pretty serious. Carl and his partner, Steve Johnson, are accused of conducting illegal testing on patients. It's not clear at this time whether the patients were aware they were being tested on. Neurotech has issued this official statement: 'Mr. Simons and Mr. Johnson were aware of the company's stance on this trial. We plan to cooperate fully with the police department during the course of this investigation.' Stay tuned to channel 4 for more on this story as it unfolds. For now, we take you to Shawn, who is live at the house of Steve Johnson."

Again, the scene changes. My charred house stands behind a man in a black blazer with a short haircut. "Thank you, Gina. As you've heard, the police suspect Steve Johnson to be involved in the illegal experimentation coming out of Neurotech. Early this morning Mr. Johnson allegedly set the house behind me on fire while his own wife and daughter were inside. It is during that commotion, according to police, that Steve was able to escape. Police say he could be armed and is considered dangerous at this time. If you see Mr. Johnson, please call the tip line flashing on the bottom of your screen. Back to you in the studio, Kim."

The studio again. "Thank you, Gina and Shawn, for those live reports. Thankfully, no one was hurt at that scene this morning."

"If no one was hurt, why the hell are you in the hospital?" My attention turns to the doorway, where Tyler has blown in like a hurricane. He looks positively panicked. His eyes are wild, his shirt is only tucked in on one side, and his face is flushed. "We've been looking all over for you." He crosses the room quickly and stands beside my bed. "Why didn't you call me? What the hell happened?"

"My Dad didn't take the news of our rendezvous very well. He tried to burn the house to the ground." I shrug, trying to make it seem better than it is.

"What part of our plan was that? I never told you to talk to him. In fact, I remember telling you that he could be dangerous. I remember telling you to stay away or to keep your Mom close."

"She was right there in the kitchen with me." I point to my Mom, who is smirking from her chair at the side of the room.

Tyler turns. The sight of my mother takes the wind out of his sails a little. "Oh. I guess it's good that you didn't do it alone. You could've been hurt." He takes a deep breath, looks back at me. "Wait, you were hurt. What happened?"

I hold up my arm, fresh plaster and all. "I broke my arm."

"Steve threw her to the floor during his escape. She also bruised herself pretty good on the right side," Mom speaks up. "I'm sorry I didn't call you, Tyler. I really need to put your number in my phone. Emma's phone is still at home."

"I'm just glad you're both safe," he concedes. "Speaking of phones, I'm going to call Bella."

I feel a flash of guilt that I didn't take care of these phone calls myself.

"Bells, I found her. We're at the Del Webb hospital, room 361." Tyler glances back at me. "Yeah, that's fine. I guess so." He shrugs. "Whatever you have to do. Alright, bye." He hits a button and sets the phone down on the table beside my bed. "She's on her way. They're actually nearby."

"They?" I ask.

Annoyance flashes across Tyler's features. "Alex was helping her look for you."

"Alex Slater?" What the hell?

"Apparently he was worried about you, too."

Is that jealousy in Tyler's voice? How do I explain that I haven't thought about Alex in a while? That I don't really care at all that he is on the way? I can't find a way to satisfactorily explain all that.

"Who's Alex?" Mom asks.

"A friend from school," I answer quickly. Hopefully Tyler notes the use of the f word.

"How come I've never heard of him?"

"I don't know. He's not really important, I guess," I explain with a shrug.

"Emma was dating him for a while…"

"But that is over," I say. "We are just friends."

An awkward silence grows in the room. I gesture to the television. "I take it things went well at the police department?"

"They took all the evidence and ran with it, so that's good. I'm not sure that it's moving as fast as the news makes it seem." Tyler's gaze flits again to my mother, like making sure she's still there, and then right back to my face. "I have to tell you something."

"Okay, go ahead."

"Emma, this whole thing with the chip and your Dad has made me realize I don't want to see you hurt."

"That's good, because I'm pretty tired of getting hurt." I try to let a little joke into my voice to ease the tension. Tyler looks so serious.

"The thought of someone hurting you was the most painful… I just couldn't deal. When I couldn't find you--"

"I'm sorry, Ty. I didn't grab my phone. We should've tried harder to contact you." I reach out and grab his hand. "I'm okay though, you can see that now."

"I know. It's just all made me realize something else."

"What's that?" I smile at him.

The door to the room opens before Tyler can say anything else. Bella bursts through the door, with Alex Slater hot on her heels. Bella makes an immediate dash to the bed and wraps me in a warm hug. "Oh my God, Emma. We were so worried." She pulls up and looks over at my Mom. "Hi Mrs. Johnson, how are you holding up?"

"I'm okay, Bella. Thank you."

"Are you okay? What the heck happened?"

"I just got injured in the shuffle with Dad… I don't really want to talk about it anymore," I say. I make a point of looking over her shoulder, reminding her that Alex doesn't know all the details.

"Hi Emma," Alex says. "I hope it's okay that I'm here. I just... I was worried about you. Bella called to ask if I had seen you. Then the news stories started and I got really worried. I met up with her to help look for you. I... um... I hope that's okay."

"Yeah, whatever. I'm fine though." Maybe he will leave. This is so uncomfortable. It's like trying to wear pants that are from two years ago; they're too short and I've just outgrown them.

"Well, I should probably head out to the waiting room. It's pretty crowded in here. I just wanted to say I'm sorry for everything... before." Alex steps a little closer to the bed, hits me with that smile. I feel the little flutter in my chest. "I didn't understand what was going on. I overreacted. I don't just want to be friends, Emma. If you're into it, I'd like to be more." He glances at Tyler, just briefly. Then his eyes are back to mine. "Let me know, okay?"

"Yeah, alright." I try to smile.

"It was nice to meet you," Alex says in Mom's direction. Then he turns and walks out of the room, pulling the door shut behind him."

"What the heck?" Bella says. "Em, that's so exciting." A huge smile lights up her entire face. She wears it for a full two seconds before it starts to fade in response to my straight face. "I think I'm missing something," she says.

My eyes dart to Tyler, standing silently against the wall beside my bed. He is wringing his hands nervously in front of him.

"I'm not exactly, um..." How do I explain this? "I don't think I'm interested anymore." I can't figure out what I'm feeling. "It's just..." I turn and focus on Tyler. "I know we've tried this a few times. I know this has failed before. But, like, we have something good. Is it something you think you want to, like, try again?" My heart is fluttering around in my throat somewhere. What am I thinking? I'm aware that Bella's eyes are as wide as spaceships over there. She probably thinks I've lost my mind.

"Are you trying to tell me that given the choice between Alex Slater and me--"

"I'd rather have you."

His entire face breaks into a soft smile as he steps back toward the bed. He takes my hand in his and squeezes it. "I love you, Em."

Whoa. That's those three words. Right there. In the room with my Mom. I can't even bring myself to turn my head and check her facial expression. My eyes are locked on Tyler's. His deep brown eyes, the ones that I can picture clearly even when he's not around. The eyes that were right there before my first kiss. The eyes that promised me safety during this whole mess. Holy crap. "I love you, too." I can't believe I didn't notice it before.

Tyler leans down, careful not to lean on me, and plants a kiss lightly on my lips. That is not the kiss I want. I'd rather share one of the toe-curling, mind-blowing, passion-igniting kisses we've had before. But I'm aware we have an audience. When he pulls away from me the first thing I see is Bella.

"Oh my God, you guys. You did not tell me this was happening!" She rushes closer and wraps Tyler in a hug. "I'm so happy for you two!"

"Excuse me." We all look to the doorway, where my doctor is standing with a clipboard and a scowl. "Sorry to interrupt." He doesn't look sorry. He looks disgusted. Tyler and Bella move even further away from the bed a little as the doctor steps closer. Mom rises. "I have a little more information for you," the doctor continues.

He crosses the room and slips an x-ray from the folder on his clipboard. He holds it up to the light near Mom. "As you can see, the ulna was fractured in your fall. This is the reason for the cast. If Emma can keep that stable enough to allow it to heal, we won't need further action. What I noticed as I reviewed the x-rays, however, is the damage elsewhere."

Oh God, there's more damage. I turn my head toward Tyler and reach up to grab his hand. I squeeze.

"You'll notice here," he points toward the image of my wrist, "it appears that the NFC chip in Emma's right wrist was cracked down the center in her fall."

Mom leans closer, squinting at the image on the x-ray. They're too far away from me. My heart pounds in my chest as wait for confirmation. "Mom?"

"Is that why this part looks darker and then there's that lightning through it?" Mom asks.

"That's not lightning. It's the crack in the chip. I've had a neurotechnologist look over this. He tells me that the chip will not be functional like that. He also explained that there is no damage in leaving it there. It's already rooted to the nervous system. He's willing to implant a new one in your left wrist--"

"No!" Tyler and I actually shout it at the same time. The poor doc looks shaken. I decide to explain. "No, thank you. I have had problems with my chip lately." I gesture to the television, where they are running the Neurotech story on a loop. "I would prefer to be chipless right now. I'm sure you understand."

The doctor shrugs. "Suit yourself. I'll send a nurse in to finish your paperwork so we can get you out of here."

"I'm going to call your grandmother." Mom steps out of the room behind the doctor, pulling the door shut behind her.

"Ty, let me see your phone." He hands it to me. I squeeze it tight and think about that kiss in the park, the one that we shared when things were dangerous. The one that curled my toes. The phone screen stays black. I try giving it a direct command, call Bella. It stays black, lifeless.

A smile breaks out, splitting my entire face. "It's fixed!"

"Technically, it's broken Em." Tyler takes his phone back, pocketing it. "But I know what you mean."

"I guess I'm the only girl with no functioning chip now." I suppose I could get used to that. My new normal.

"That's okay. I still love you." The words drip with emotion. Tyler rests on his right arm and leans closer. I close the gap, kissing him deeply. Hopefully it curls his toes as much as mine.

Yeah, I could get used to this.

About the Author

Tabatha Shipley lives in Arizona with her awesome husband, two amazing kids, and weird dog. When she's not writing she's probably reading or cooking. Although not usually at the same time, because that can get messy. She can often be found on social media talking about books.

Check out her website where you can find information about new releases, a blog, and all her social media handles.

https://tabathashipleybooks.com/

Thank you for supporting independent authors. If you enjoyed this story, please leave a review.

Made in the USA
Middletown, DE
21 April 2022

64594086R00123